THE GREAT CHRISTMAS TREE MYSTERY

JAMEY MOODY

As an independent author, reviews are greatly appreciated

The Great Christmas Tree Mystery

Edited: Kat Jackson

Thank you for purchasing my book. I hope you enjoy the story.

If you'd like to stay updated on future releases, you can visit my website or sign up for my mailing list here: www.jameymoodyauthor.com.

I'd love to hear from you! Email me at jameymoodyauthor@gmail.com.

Created with Vellum

CONTENTS

ALSO BY JAMEY MOODY

Live This Love

The Your Way Series:

Finding Home

Finding Family

Finding Forever

It Takes A Miracle

One Little Yes

The Lovers Landing Series

Where Secrets Are Safe

No More Secrets

And The Truth Is...

The Great Christmas Tree Mystery

PROLOGUE

The small town of Santa Junction has always been a magical place. Just the name alone conjures visions of jolly ole Saint Nick. It was thought to be one of the places around the world that Santa met his elves to restock his sleigh. Surely he couldn't carry all the presents for all the children in one big sleigh. There were places in different parts of the world like the junction—other stops along the paths of his route. Santa Junction was the perfect out of the way place to reload the sleigh to service the New England section of the United States.

Three years ago a most curious thing began to happen. On Thursday nights in early December, the shops on the town square would stay open late so the townspeople could shop and enjoy the festive atmosphere. Holiday music played through speakers and the stores were decorated with festive lights and greenery. A booth was brought in that sold hot chocolate and coffee for those cold nights while people meandered through the shops.

On one particularly cold night, after the stores had closed and the people were warm in their homes, a car drove through the square and then stopped. It backed up and then shone its lights on a sad little tree in the square's green space.

A person got out and did the strangest thing. They began to decorate the tree with a string of lights. After the lights were secure they began to hang ornaments from the scraggly little branches. As each bauble was placed on the tree something magical began to happen. It was as if the little tree began to fill with Christmas cheer. The branches became fuller, the tree stood taller, and the needles took on a bright green color.

This tree decorating slowly transformed a sad little sapling into a beautiful Christmas tree. The final touch was when they placed a star on the tip of its top branch. This magical elf that was dressed as a regular human then turned the lights on and backed away. The twinkling bulbs lit up this elf's face that was covered with joy.

The next morning when the town began to wake they noticed there was no longer a sad little tree in the town square. A festively decorated Christmas tree had taken its place. Holiday cheer spread through the town when anyone mentioned the "tree on the square."

Over the next two weeks four other trees in different parts of town were magically decorated. Santa Junction was alive with Christmas cheer and as word spread of the decorated trees appearing around town, people from all over came to see, and The Great Christmas Tree Mystery was born.

1

"It's definitely Christmas now!" Rita exclaimed as Noelle Winters walked into the Santa Junction newspaper office, also known as the Santa Sentinel.

"Hi Rita." Noelle smiled, shaking her head.

"I was just telling Sasha about the Great Christmas Tree Mystery that comes around this time of year," said Rita. She turned to find a woman standing in the doorway to a hall that disappeared into the back of the building. "Let me introduce you, Noelle."

"You're Sasha Solomon," Noelle said, tilting her head.

"I am," said Sasha, walking toward the counter that separated Noelle from the open room. She held out her hand and Noelle didn't hesitate to take it in hers.

"Noelle Winters," she said calmly with a smile. "Nice to meet you," she added, still holding Sasha's hand.

Sasha smiled and looked into the most beautiful green eyes she'd ever seen.

Rita looked on, smiling at both of them. "Aren't we lucky, Noelle. Sasha joined our scandal sheet last month," she said.

Noelle looked surprised. “I’d say so, Rita.”

“What I want to know is why is it all of a sudden Christmas because you are here?” quizzed Sasha, arching an eyebrow.

Rita chuckled. “Noelle doesn’t come home very often, but you can always count on a visit at Christmas.”

Noelle smiled and quickly changed the subject. “What’s this about the Christmas Tree Mystery?”

“You know what I’m talking about.” Rita looked at her pointedly. “For the last few years at different times during the holiday season a tree will suddenly appear all decorated for Christmas. And to this day no one has claimed responsibility.”

Noelle nodded. “Oh, *that* great Christmas tree mystery,” she deadpanned.

Rita gave her a stern glance and turned to Sasha. “It’s rather magical because it happens at random times and to random trees. It brings the town together and spreads Christmas cheer.”

“It’s done anonymously?” asked Sasha.

“Yes. I think you should use that investigative instinct of yours and find out who is doing it,” said Rita.

“Why would you do that?” asked Noelle.

Rita turned to Noelle. “Because I want to know who it is. And because we want to say thank you.”

“We?” Noelle asked, raising her eyebrows.

“The town.”

“Maybe they’re staying anonymous for a reason,” suggested Noelle.

“Well, duh,” chided Rita.

Sasha couldn’t hold in her laughter at the exchange going on in front of her. She’d come to this small out-of-the-way, Christmas-named town for moments just like this. Her illustrious career spanned twenty-five years in investigative journalism. She'd been all over the world reporting on wars, natural disasters, politics, and popular topics of the moment until it had become too much. At forty-eight she wanted to take a breath and put the horror she'd witnessed off and on through her career behind her. And Santa Junction had so far provided that needed break.

"Has the Christmas tree bandit struck yet this year?" Noelle asked playfully.

"He's not a bandit," Rita huffed. "He's putting them up, not stealing them."

"Excuse me!" Noelle grinned, holding up her hands.

"To answer your question, no," Rita said. "There has not been a decorated tree yet this year."

"Maybe it's been a tough year and this do-gooder has no Christmas cheer left," suggested Noelle, obviously enjoying this banter with Rita.

"Maybe this he is a she," offered Sasha, entering the conversation.

Rita looked at her, eyes wide. "See there! Her investigator juices are beginning to flow."

Noelle looked at Sasha with a smile playing at the corner of her mouth.

Sasha gazed into those sparkling green eyes and her investigative senses began to ping. Was there a secret hiding behind those emerald jewels?

"You could help her," Rita said to Noelle.

Noelle tore her eyes away from Sasha's and asked, "What's that? Help who?"

"You could help Sasha solve this merry mystery."

Noelle laughed. "Why would an accomplished journalist like Ms. Solomon need my help? And how in the world *could* I help?" she added.

"You grew up here! You know this town," said Rita.

Noelle shook her head. "I may have grown up here, Rita, but I haven't lived here in over twenty years!"

"That doesn't matter. You come home every Christmas. You know this town," she said matter-of-factly. "It's the neighborly thing to do."

"I'm sure Ms. Solomon–" began Noelle.

"Please, call me Sasha," she said with a smile.

"Sasha." Noelle nodded. "I'm sure you have plenty of other stories to work on and you certainly don't need my help."

Sasha tilted her head and pursed her lips. She was beginning to enjoy Noelle's efforts to escape Rita's urgings and could see her beginning to squirm just a bit. "How about you share your contact information so if I do need help I'll know where to find you?" she suggested.

Noelle's eyebrows raised once again in surprise. "I guess I could do that."

Sasha smiled at her ingenious way to get Noelle's number. Not that she could imagine ever using it, but it was amusing nonetheless.

Noelle took her phone from her back pocket and unlocked it. She handed it to Sasha who then put her number in and sent a text to herself.

"There you go," she said, handing her phone back to Noelle.

"Thanks, I think," she said hesitantly. "It was nice to meet you." She nodded at Sasha. "Bye." She turned and walked out the door, but then came right back in.

"I forgot the reason I came in the first place. Nick asked me to drop these by," she said, handing Rita a folder.

She looked inside and nodded.

"Nick?" said Sasha.

"Nick is my brother."

"Nick and Noelle. Wow, your folks must have loved Christmas," commented Sasha.

"You could say that. My mom's name was Holly, dad was Chris." Noelle shrugged.

Sasha narrowed her eyes. "You're kidding me, right?" she said skeptically.

"She speaks the truth," said Rita, chuckling.

"Bye now," said Noelle, walking out the door once again.

Rita noticed Sasha watching Noelle through the storefront windows. "She bats for your team, you know."

"What?" Sasha said, tearing her eyes away looking at Rita.

"She's gay! Loves the ladies! Just like you."

"Oh," said Sasha. "I came here to get away from drama, remember, Rita?"

"That doesn't mean you can't have a little fun."

Sasha considered Rita's words and thought that Noelle Winters would most certainly be fun, but she doubted *she* would be. There were too many scars she carried from seemingly casual affairs for her to be any fun. But still. She turned and walked down the hall.

"Mission accomplished," Rita said out loud. "It's time for you to come home, Noelle Winters, and maybe Sasha Solomon is just the person to get you here."

2

Noelle walked into her brother's store and nodded to several of the sales associates. She knew most of them since they had worked for Nick for years now. Her brother was one of the good guys. He treated his workers fairly and paid a decent wage. The community was important to him and he tried to make it a better place and helped whenever he was needed.

She continued to the back of the store and through his open office door. "You didn't tell me Sasha Solomon was working for the newspaper!"

"She hasn't been here long," replied Nick. "Did Rita introduce you?"

Noelle furrowed her brow. "Yeah, she did."

Nick chuckled. "She couldn't wait to introduce you to her."

"Why?"

"Because you're gay, dumbass. You do know Sasha Solomon is gay, right?"

Noelle looked at him, exasperated. The award-winning investigative journalist was not only known for reporting from around the world. "Yes I know she's gay. She's one of the most prominent lesbians in the world. That's why I was so surprised to see her at our little paper."

"Supposedly she wanted to get away from the stress and travel."

"Hmm," murmured Noelle.

"Rita thinks you should go out with her. That's why she couldn't wait for you to get home."

"Why would I do that? I never go out with anyone when I'm home," said Noelle, bewildered.

"Exactly. Maybe you should. It might be fun for you," said Nick.

"Rita wants her to investigate what she's calling The Great Christmas Tree Mystery." Noelle rolled her eyes.

"Oh," said Nick.

"Yeah, oh," parroted Noelle.

"Hello," someone called from outside the door. Sasha Solomon appeared in the doorway. When she saw Noelle her smile widened. "Oh, hello again."

"Hi," Noelle said shyly.

"I hope I'm not interrupting. Your sales person told me I'd find you in your office," she said to Nick.

"You're not interrupting. I hear you've met my sister," said Nick, looking over at Noelle.

"I have." Sasha nodded at Noelle. "Rita made sure of it," she added with a chuckle.

Noelle laughed. "Of course she did."

"What can I help you with, Sasha?" asked Nick.

"Well, I thought I'd purchase a Christmas tree. My house could use a little cheer and Rita assured me this was the best place to get one," said Sasha.

Nick laughed. "Yes, this would be the best place because it's the only place you can get a live tree in town. My top sales person would be glad to help you." Nick gestured towards Noelle.

Sasha looked at Noelle. "You work here?"

"I fill in for Nick's workers some evenings at the tree lot. I'd be glad to help you," said Noelle, walking towards the door.

"See you later, sis," Nick called to Noelle as they walked out.

Noelle waved without turning around and led Sasha to the tree lot.

"That's nice of you to help out while you're home," said Sasha.

"This store has been in our family for years. My grandfather started it," said Noelle. "I don't mind helping so the workers can spend time with their families during the holidays."

They walked along and were among the trees when Sasha asked, "How long are you here for?"

Noelle smiled. "A month."

"Wow! That's a vacation!"

Noelle chuckled. "Rita didn't tell you how long I'm home?"

Sasha laughed and nodded. "She may have mentioned it. But she didn't say what you do."

They stopped to look at a tree. "Now this is a nice one. You can't go wrong with a fir," said Noelle.

"It is nice." Sasha reached out, touching the needles.

"We have probably been in some of the same places," Noelle said cryptically.

Sasha looked up at her. "How so?"

"My work takes me into disaster areas and other places where humanitarian relief efforts are needed," said Noelle.

"Really," she said, looking into Noelle's eyes.

Noelle felt like Sasha was trying to see into her soul with those warm brown eyes. "You know how relief organizations go into an area to help?" Noelle asked.

Sasha nodded, holding Noelle's gaze.

"Oftentimes there are so many agencies and organizations there that the people affected don't know what to do. I go in and they talk to me first and I send them to where they can get the help they need. It makes the process easier and gets the people in a better situation sooner."

"I see. So I would go in and report what's happening and get attention on the event, whether it's an earthquake, miners trapped, terrorist attack, or something else. And then you come in behind that and do the actual work to help the people." She continued to stare at Sasha as she spoke. "I've always wondered what happens to them after I leave," she said quietly.

Noelle's eyes were focused on Sasha and she could see her remembering something as she spoke.

Sasha shook her head and smiled at Noelle. "No wonder you're off for a month. What you do is hard. The public doesn't realize that."

Noelle smiled at her. "As you know, my mom was crazy about Christmas," she began. "She always made Christmas special for a struggling family. Mom was a school counselor and knew which families were having a hard time. Anyway, she taught me by example that we are all here together and should help one another. That translated into my work life."

Noelle watched Sasha as she looked at her and seemed to choose her words carefully. "You said we were in the same places, so you know what I used to do?"

"I do," said Noelle. "And I was very surprised to see you at the newspaper."

Sasha smiled and nodded. "May I ask you something?'

"Of course." Noelle nodded.

"Does it ever get to you? Does it become too much?" she asked seriously.

Noelle nodded. "Every place I go."

Sasha exhaled a breath, then whispered, "I had to get away."

Noelle barely heard her. "I get that. Why do you think I come home every year for a month at Christmas? I'm always so tired and drained, but my mom would fill me up with her over-the-top Christmas spirit and off I'd go."

"Would?"

Noelle smiled sadly. "Yeah, she died three years ago."

"Oh Noelle," Sasha said, reaching out and putting her hand on Noelle's forearm. "I'm so sorry."

Noelle swallowed the lump in her throat and forced a cheerful smile on her face. "Enough tragedy and gloom. Selecting the perfect tree is a happy time."

"Can I let you in on a little secret?" Sasha asked, following Noelle's lead.

"Your secret is safe with me," Noelle said, leaning in a little closer.

"I've never really chosen a Christmas tree before."

Noelle stood straighter and her brows flew up her forehead. "You've never picked out a tree?"

"Shh," Sasha said, holding her finger to her mouth. "Someone else always did it for me or I was someplace else in the world and didn't have one."

Noelle looked at Sasha kindly and smiled. "Well then, we will find an extra special tree that is only for you."

"Is that how it works?" Sasha said, leaning in closer to Noelle as they walked towards the back of the lot.

"Oh yes. Most of the time the tree picks you," said Noelle with a twinkle in her eye. This was becoming a nice way to spend the afternoon, she thought as she looked over at Sasha who was eyeing each tree with concentration.

"Do they call to you or what because I'm not getting any vibes," said Sasha as she continued to the next row.

"Sort of." Noelle smiled as they walked onto the last row. "You'll know when you know."

"Okay," said Sasha as she followed along.

They both stopped at the last tree in the last row. It was a small tree with a few branches that didn't quite look symmetrical. There were also a few spots that weren't filled out.

They both stared at the tree and then looked at each other.

"This is it," said Sasha with a grin beginning to cover her face.

"This is definitely it." Noelle matched her grin.

"I mean, it isn't perfect. But with a little love..." said Sasha, still smiling at the tree.

"Love will make it perfect," said Noelle quietly.

"So what now?" asked Sasha.

"Now..." Noelle looked around. "Do you have a car or SUV?"

"Car," answered Sasha.

Noelle looked at her watch and then smiled at Sasha. "We are all about service, so I'll tell you what. We close in an hour and I can use Nick's truck to deliver your tree."

"That would be great," said Sasha with excitement.

"Do you have a tree stand?"

"Uh." She scrunched up her face. "If I did I wouldn't know where it was."

Noelle chuckled. "I'll bring one with me and help you set it up."

"I really appreciate it. I didn't realize there was this much to it." She shrugged.

"I'm happy to do it. I'll need an address to go with the phone number you put in my phone," Noelle said.

Sasha pulled out her phone and texted the address to Noelle.

Noelle's phone pinged in her back pocket. "Hmm, I wonder who that is?" she said playfully.

"I guess you'll have to read it and see," Sasha said, playing along.

Noelle looked at the text and nodded.

"I'm thinking you know the street since you grew up here."

"I do," Noelle said. "I'll be there in an hour or so."

They turned and started to walk back towards the parking lot and Sasha stopped. "You will bring the right tree, right?"

Noelle grabbed her chest and gasped. "Of course I will."

"I mean you didn't mark it or anything and I wouldn't want someone else taking it because it clearly needs to be with me."

"That tree has your name all over it. Trust me."

Sasha eyed her and said, "I guess I'll have to." Then she grinned. "Thanks again for delivering it."

"You're welcome."

Sasha walked to her car and Noelle went back through the trees to wrap up that special one.

"Hey!" Sasha called to Noelle as she ran to the back of the lot. "I didn't pay you." She stopped in front of Noelle, catching her breath.

"Oh yeah," said Noelle. "Consider it a welcome to Santa Junction gift."

"What? No! How much is it?"

Noelle leaned in and held her hand to her mouth like she was telling a secret. "I don't get to work here very often, so please let me do this. It's what my grandfather would do," she said with a youthful grin. "Besides, it's your first time. My treat."

Sasha was speechless and the smile on her face made Noelle's stomach flutter with butterflies.

"Okay," she said hesitantly. "I'll see you at my house."

Noelle smiled and nodded and then walked off before Sasha changed her mind.

3

Sasha went home but couldn't get Noelle Winters off her mind. At times she seemed to have a deep sadness in her eyes and Sasha understood that well, having learned what she did for work. Going to places where people were in desperate need of help for whatever reason was hard on the spirit. Sasha saw it nearly every day in her job and then she left and went on to the next disaster or hot news story. But Noelle stayed and helped. She did the true humanitarian work.

Those twinkling green eyes weren't always sad, though. With that dark red hair and playful wit, Sasha had found her heart beating fast more than once when she was around Noelle. The last thing she wanted or intended when she moved here was to think about women. But Noelle had an air of mystery about her and it would be fun to make a friend for the holidays. She'd be leaving anyway so what could it hurt?

She quickly changed into leggings and an oversized pullover hoodie. After a quick survey of her living room, she decided to put the tree in front of her living room window.

When the lights were on at night it would be visible from the street. If this sudden infusion of Christmas spirit continued maybe she'd even put up outdoor lights.

It didn't take her long to move a couple pieces of furniture around so the area would be ready for the tree. She caught herself smiling at the thought of seeing Noelle again. That would be three times today and she'd just met the woman. Before she could contemplate this she saw a pickup pull into her driveway. Noelle hopped out, heading to the back of it.

Sasha opened the front door and walked out onto the porch. "You found me?"

Noelle looked up at her. "Were you lost?"

"Ha ha," she said, walking to the back of the truck.

Noelle smiled at her. "I have an under-appreciated Christmas tree that can't wait to adorn your home."

Sasha clapped her hands together like an excited child. "I can't believe I'm so excited about a Christmas tree."

"What do you mean? You should be. They bring instant cheer," Noelle said, grabbing the tree and scooting it to the edge of the tailgate. Then she took a tree stand and handed it to Sasha. She grabbed the tree by the trunk and then her other hand disappeared into the tree. "Lead the way."

"This way. Can I help?" she asked as she hurried up to the porch, not wanting to be in the way.

"I've got it," Noelle said, following behind.

"It's just inside here. I've already made a place for it," said Sasha, stepping into the living room.

Noelle followed her inside and stood the tree up. It was just a little taller than her, but not quite as tall as Sasha.

"Do you have a towel we could put down to put the tree stand on? You'll have to water the tree occasionally and that will protect your floor just in case."

Sasha disappeared into the hallway and came back with a towel. “In case of what? In case I spill water?”

Noelle chuckled. “I didn’t say that. Just, in case.”

Sasha met those twinkling green eyes and her heart fluttered momentarily.

“Could you hold this while I get the stand ready?” Noelle asked.

“Sure.”Sasha reached her hand into the tree where Noelle was holding it. Their hands brushed for just a moment and their eyes met and held.

Noelle reached for the towel and spread it out on the floor. She put the tree stand down and made sure the opening was wide enough before she stood back up.

“I sawed off the bottom of the tree to make sure it was level. Hopefully it will slide right in and stay put. Here we go,” she said. “Fingers crossed.”

She reached for the tree and they both guided it toward the tree stand. Noelle picked it up slightly and set it through the ring. “Can you hold it while I tighten the stand?”

“Sure thing. I’ve got it,” said Sasha.

Noelle crawled under the tree and tightened the bolts into the tree trunk. She rolled over on her back and looked up at Sasha. “Okay, very gently let go and let’s see if it will stand on its own.”

Sasha did as Noelle said, but she couldn’t keep from looking down at Noelle splayed out on her living room floor. When their eyes met through the branches she didn’t look away.

“Did you let go?” Noelle asked, gazing up at her.

Sasha nodded slowly. “I did.”

They stayed like this for a moment and then the spell was broken when the tree started to lean. Sasha quickly grabbed it before it fell over on top of Noelle.

"Oops," laughed Noelle. She adjusted one of the bolts and said from under the tree, "Try again."

This time the tree stayed upright and Sasha said, "I think it's safe for you to come out now."

"If only that were true for everyone," Noelle said, climbing out from under the tree.

"What?" said Sasha.

"Coming out," said Noelle.

"Oh!" exclaimed Sasha. "Right." Maybe there was a story there.

"Okay." Noelle clapped her hands. "She's all ready for decorations."

Sasha stood back and admired the new addition to her living room. "You know, I think I'm going to enjoy it for a while in all its naked glory."

Noelle stood beside her and looked over at the tree, eyebrows raised, nodding. Then she turned to Sasha. "You don't have decorations do you?"

Sasha met her gaze. "I do. I simply don't know where they are," she said sheepishly.

Noelle tilted her head. "I'll be right back."

She walked out the front door, went to the pickup and came back in with a sack. She took out two boxes of lights, several ornaments, and a star for the top of the tree.

"What's all this?" exclaimed Sasha.

"I thought you might need a few things since you haven't been here long. I didn't bring very many ornaments because you should choose those yourself," explained Noelle. "But I brought you this little one that says Santa Junction, a merry Santa Claus, and the cutest snowman you'll ever see."

"I'm beginning to think your mom wasn't the only one that loved Christmas," Sasha said, touched by Noelle's generosity.

"I don't know what happened. I blame it on your Christmas tree. It somehow gave me a dose of much needed Christmas spirit," said Noelle, smiling at Sasha.

Sasha watched Noelle unpack the Christmas goodies and then those eyes met hers and she was enchanted. "What are we waiting for? Will you help me decorate?"

"Are you sure?" asked Noelle.

"Of course I am. I'll knock this magical little tree over if I try to put those lights on by myself," said Sasha.

Together they began to string the lights on the tree. "You weren't kidding when you said full service, were you?" Sasha laughed.

Noelle laughed. "I'm telling you, it's this magical little tree."

They finished with the lights and Noelle handed the ornaments to Sasha to place on the tree.

"You're right, this is the cutest little snowman," Sasha said, putting it right in front.

"All that's left is the star." Noelle handed it to her. "Wait. I'll hold the tree while you put it on."

Sasha waited and once Noelle was holding the tree she reached up and pushed the star down on the top branch.

They both stepped back and admired their work.

"Well, turn on those lights, you merry little elf," said Noelle, chuckling.

Sasha laughed and reached behind the tree and plugged the lights into the socket.

"Wow," said Noelle.

Sasha stood next to her and marveled at the tree, her tree. It looked so much better than it had in the lot that afternoon.

"Would you look at what a little love can do?" she said, delighted. "I can't believe it's the same tree."

"Imagine how good it's going to look by Christmas," said Noelle. "Oh, I forgot to water it."

"I'll get some." Sasha walked into the kitchen. She came back out with the water and carefully knelt down and poured it into the tree stand. "There we go."

She took a deep breath and exhaled. "It makes my house smell so good."

Noelle inhaled deeply. "It does."

"I love it," said Sasha. She turned to Noelle. "Thank you so much."

"You're very welcome," said Noelle. "You know, the stores around the square stay open late on Thursdays during the holidays."

"I know."

"Would you want to join me for a cup of hot chocolate and maybe we could pick up a few more ornaments for this magical tree?" said Noelle.

"I'd love to, but you have to let me buy the hot chocolate as a way to say thanks for all you've done," said Sasha, nodding towards the Christmas tree.

"I guess I could let you do that." Noelle smiled.

"And where's that invoice you were supposed to bring me?"

Noelle narrowed her eyes. "At the store."

Sasha chuckled and nodded. "I'll go by tomorrow."

Noelle shrugged.

"Let me get my coat."

4

They walked out the front door and Noelle said, "If you don't mind riding in a work truck I'll drive, but I can't promise you won't pick up a little dirt."

"A little dirt never bothered me," Sasha said, walking around to the passenger side. "You know how it is in remote places; you never feel clean."

"I know, there always seems to be dust, no matter the climate," said Noelle, starting the pickup.

"What do you usually do when you're home, besides working at the store?"

"I spend time with my brother and his family. His daughter Belle is the only one that lives here now, but the others come in for Christmas. I have a few friends I see, too."

"That's nice. I don't have much family and I think that's why I stayed with the job as long as I did. It also doesn't lend itself to successful relationships. At least it didn't for me."

Noelle glanced over at her. "I know what you mean. I seemed to always be gone when a girlfriend needed me and they got tired of that."

"Exactly," said Sasha.

Noelle found a parking place when they neared the town square. "It looks like several folks had the same idea we did."

"That's good though. Santa Junction at its finest, spreading Christmas cheer."

"You're really getting into this small town spirit, aren't you?"

"I wanted a change so why not embrace it?" Sasha shrugged, walking next to Noelle. "Do you ever think of moving back?"

"Not really. I know I won't do this job forever, but honestly the town doesn't seem the same without my mom." Noelle stopped walking.

"It must be hard coming home then," Sasha said kindly. She turned around when she noticed Noelle wasn't beside her. "Are you all right?"

"I'm surprised I admitted that out loud," she said.

Sasha smiled warmly. "Sometimes it's easier to say things to people that don't know you as well."

"I guess."

"Or maybe it's because I understand where you've been as far as your job goes," offered Sasha.

Noelle smiled at her. "Maybe. How about that hot chocolate?" she said, changing the subject.

They walked over to a little gingerbread decorated hut and Noelle ordered two cups. She turned to Sasha and asked, "Marshmallows?"

"Of course, is there any other way?"

Noelle chuckled and handed her the steamy beverage. They both held their cups up and let the aroma and warmth blanket their faces before trying a tiny sip.

"Mmm, delicious," said Sasha.

"Let's go this way." Noelle led her past a couple of shops

as Christmas music played through speakers hung in the trees in the green area inside of the square.

They ambled down the wide sidewalk, stopping to look into the storefront windows. If something caught their eye they'd go in and meander through the store. Noelle stopped several times to say hello to people that welcomed her home for the holidays. She started to introduce Sasha, but most of the folks knew who she was.

"You still know a lot of people here," commented Sasha after a chat with one of the store owners.

"And you *already* know a lot of people here," said Noelle.

"This is a friendly town," said Sasha.

"It can be, but I'm sure everyone is excited to have the famous Sasha Solomon in our midst."

"I don't know about that," Sasha said modestly.

"I do." Noelle eyed her. "Let's go in here. I think we might find something for your tree."

"Hey Aunt Noelle."

Noelle turned around and smiled. "Hi Belle," she said when the younger woman stopped in front of her. "Belle, this is Sasha Solomon."

"I met you at the high school," said Sasha with a friendly smile.

"You did," said Belle, nodding. "What are you two up to?"

"Your aunt sold and delivered me a Christmas tree. Now we're getting a few ornaments," Sasha said merrily.

Belle looked at Noelle. "My aunt has a way with Christmas trees."

Sasha noticed Noelle's eyes widened at her niece. "I'd agree with you because she brought me a magical tree," said Sasha.

"I'm sure she did," said Belle, grinning at her aunt. "I'll

see you later tonight, Aunt Noelle. It was nice seeing you, Sasha. Have fun."

Belle continued down the sidewalk and Noelle held the door open for them to go inside the store. They walked to a display of Christmas ornaments and looked them over. After a few moments Noelle said, "I like this one." She held up a rainbow with holly sprinkled over the top of it.

"I love it," said Sasha.

"It's my treat. Welcome to Santa Junction, if you will," said Noelle with a big smile.

"You already brought me those others and the tree."

"Yes, but I know you're going to pay for them tomorrow. This is from me," said Noelle.

Sasha let out a breath. "Okay. Thank you, I appreciate it."

Noelle tipped her head slightly.

Sasha held up the ornament she was holding and showed it to Noelle. It was a hand painted ball with two people on it. They were shown from behind gazing at a tree in the forest decorated for Christmas. "If I'm looking at it, I see two women."

Noelle looked at it and said, "I do too."

"It reminds me of the Great Christmas Tree Mystery Rita was telling me about when you walked into the newspaper office today."

Noelle looked at it. "The trees aren't really in the middle of a forest."

"Yes, but they are trees decorated in various places outside, right?" asked Sasha.

"That's true," said Noelle.

"You know why Rita was so excited to introduce us, don't you?" asked Sasha.

Noelle chuckled. "I do."

Sasha liked Santa Junction, but it had been a big adjustment moving here. In the beginning she'd come here with no expectations on how long she'd stay and that hadn't changed in the almost two months since she'd arrived. She was trying to unpack and make her house feel more permanent, but Noelle had helped her see the homey side of Santa Junction in just one evening. No one else had done that.

"Would you want to go to dinner with me?" she suddenly asked Noelle.

Noelle looked up at her and tilted her head.

"It would be a gift to Rita if we did," coaxed Sasha.

A smile played at the corner of Noelle's mouth. "You want me to go to dinner with you as a gift to Rita?" she asked, amused.

"No," Sasha said. "I added that in case you wanted to say no."

"You're not confident that I would say yes?"

Sasha studied her for a moment before answering. "Honestly, I haven't wanted to go out with anyone in a long time. But I've just met you today and we've put up a Christmas tree, decorated it and spent a lovely evening sipping hot chocolate and buying more ornaments for said tree." She smiled and continued. "That magical tree has connected us. Why not spend more time together and give Rita a gift at the same time."

"I'm not about to mess with magic. I'd love to have dinner with you," Noelle said, returning her smile. "Just so you know, I'd have gone out with you even if you hadn't mentioned Rita."

"That's certainly good for my confidence."

"It's hard for me to believe you are lacking in confidence," said Noelle as they began to walk to the front of the store to pay for the ornaments.

Sasha and Noelle laid their ornaments on the counter. Sasha turned to Noelle. "Are you sure you won't let me pay for yours?"

"I'm sure."

Sasha paid for her ornaments and stepped aside to wait on Noelle.

"Hi Mr. Hinson," Noelle said as he entered her purchases into the computer.

"It's good to see you, Noelle. Did you mean to buy two of these? Didn't you already buy these earlier?" he asked, holding up two of the rainbow ornaments.

"Yes sir," she assured him.

Sasha looked on at this exchange and thought that Noelle was probably buying one for her tree too.

Once outside the store they walked towards the truck. Sasha brought them back to their earlier conversation. "I am very confident in my job because I know what I'm doing. But asking someone out is a whole different thing."

"Anyone would want to go out with you! You're a smart, successful, well-known journalist," Noelle said earnestly.

"Thank you for saying that, but I don't want just anyone to go out with me. I want you," Sasha said, nudging Noelle's shoulder with her own.

"Well," Noelle paused. "I hope I can live up to whatever Rita told you about me because I know she gave you an earful."

Sasha chuckled. "Let's just say we'll have plenty to talk about."

Noelle looked down, shaking her head. "Oh no."

5

After Noelle took Sasha home, she drove across town and pulled into her brother's driveway. When her mother died they sold the family house and built a tiny house at the back of Nick's property. His house sat on an acre of land and he built the little cottage especially for her so she'd have her own place when she came to visit. Noelle loved the little bungalow and the fact that she had privacy when she wanted it or she could hang out in the main house with her family.

Her niece's car was also in the driveway so she went into the backyard and instead of going to her place she went in through the back door and found her family sitting around the kitchen table. All the major decisions and family discussions had been held around the kitchen table while she was growing up. That very table now sat in Nick and Lisa's kitchen.

"Look who finally made it," said Nick, grinning at his sister.

Noelle looked at him and tilted her head. "Was I supposed to be here for something?"

"How was your date?" asked Nick.

"I haven't gone yet," replied Noelle with confusion on her face.

"What?" he asked.

"What?" Noelle parroted.

"Belle was just telling us that she saw you downtown with Sasha Solomon and Nick shared that you sold her a Christmas tree today," said Noelle's sister-in-law, Lisa.

"And she delivered it," added Nick. "Now what do you mean about a date?"

"What did you mean about a date?"

"Belle said you were drinking hot chocolate and shopping with Sasha. I thought it might be an impromptu date."

"Oh!" said Noelle. She paused and could feel her cheeks becoming red. "She asked me to go to dinner with her."

"Ohhh!" exclaimed Lisa. "Surely you said yes."

Noelle nodded, a smile growing on her face. She sat down and looked around the table. She loved these people, but they enjoyed teasing her way too much. She directed her attention to Lisa and said, "She has a car. So I offered to drop the Christmas tree by in the pickup."

"You are such a thoughtful person," Nick said, nodding with fake sincerity.

Noelle flipped him off and Lisa and Belle both laughed.

"That doesn't explain how you ended up at the square with her," said Belle.

"She couldn't find her decorations. I have a feeling she hasn't unpacked everything yet. Anyway, I invited her for hot chocolate and we stopped and bought a few ornaments."

"To go with the lights and ornaments I saw you put in the truck along with her Christmas tree," said Nick.

"She'll be by tomorrow to pay for them!" Noelle exclaimed.

"I don't care about that," Nick said, chuckling. "You were being thoughtful and I mean it this time."

Noelle shrugged.

"What about this dinner?" asked Lisa.

Noelle smiled, remembering how tentative Sasha sounded when she asked her. "We were having a nice time. She asked me to dinner. That's all there is to it."

"Uh huh," said Nick. "What about her investigation of the Christmas tree mystery?"

When Lisa and Belle looked at her, seeming to be confused, she explained. "Rita told her about the trees. She's made it into the Great Christmas Tree Mystery and she's trying to get Sasha to use her investigative skills to find out who is doing it."

"Hmm, that could be troublesome," said Lisa.

"I think it would be a great reason for Auntie Noelle to keep her close. That way you'll know what she finds out," said Belle.

"Oh, you wouldn't want to go out with her because she's a beautiful, interesting woman, would you?" teased Lisa.

"Have you seen my beautiful, interesting aunt?" said Belle, putting her arm around Noelle. "That's why she asked you out."

"All these beautiful interesting people are making me dizzy. What I want to know is how you're going to hide the fact that *you* are the one that decorates the trees," said Nick.

"My helper and I are going to be careful, just as we have been for the last three years," said Noelle. "And we have a job tonight."

"That's why I'm here."

"Well, you know how the first tree we decorate is always

on the square," she began. "Last year we did the one on the north side which was perfect because it's where the two main roads meet."

"It made me smile every time I drove by," said Lisa.

"I think everyone will expect that one to be decorated again and the cameras at the front door of the courthouse are pointed right at it. So, I found the cutest little pine tree on the east side that we're going to decorate tonight."

"What about cameras?" asked Nick.

"It's a small tree and won't take more than five minutes to throw the lights on, put the star on the top and hang a few ornaments."

"But if you're on camera they'll recognize you," said Lisa.

"Nope. We're wearing hoodies and these." Noelle reached into her backpack and pulled out two Christmas masks. "Aren't these the cutest little masks you've ever seen?"

One was a merry Santa and the other was a happy elf. "You choose," she said to Belle.

"Perfect," said Nick. "But what about your car?"

"I have that figured out too. All the decorations are in a bag that we will hide behind that bigger tree near the east courthouse entrance. We'll take Lisa's car and I'll jump out when we turn the corner and hide the bag. Then I'll walk across the lawn and jump back in the car when Belle turns the next corner. We'll park a couple of blocks away and walk in. It's already dark, there's no moon and we'll stay away from the streetlights. Once we're done, we'll walk back to the car and come home." Noelle sat back and let her family digest all she'd told them. She could see each of them playing the scenario through in their minds.

"Aren't there cameras on all sides of the courthouse?" asked Nick.

"Yes, but there happens to be a small blind spot at the corners. That's where we'll walk in."

"And you don't think they'll be able to recognize the car?" asked Lisa.

"They may see me get out, but they won't see me get back in because Belle is going to go down another block before she comes back up the other street. The cameras on the courthouse only see that first block."

Belle nodded. "I think it will work."

Noelle looked at her watch and said, "Let's wait another hour and make sure everyone will be cleared out and the stores locked up."

"Thanks for letting me help again this year, Aunt Noelle," said Belle. "Mimi would love this!"

"She may not be around to deliver Christmas cheer like she always did, but you are," said Nick, pinning his sister with a look. "She'd be proud."

"She always made sure the families she helped never knew it was her, so that's why we can't let anyone know. Right?" Noelle looked around the room.

Everyone nodded.

"Are you worried about Sasha finding out?" asked Lisa. "She is world renowned for her investigative skills. Finding out who is decorating trees in a sleepy little New York town is probably nothing for her."

"We'll see." Noelle had a sly smile on her face. When she'd first come home, she'd felt dread instead of Christmas cheer because she missed her mom so much. Sasha Solomon had suddenly made this holiday much more interesting and she was actually starting to feel a bit of Christmas cheer.

"May we borrow your car?" she asked Lisa.

"Of course. Even if they ID it I don't think they'll suspect the lead detective at the Santa Junction police department," she said, grinning. "Hmm, maybe I should drive you in my work car."

Noelle chuckled. "No. I don't want you to have to lie for us."

"Okay. I'm going home to change," said Belle.

"I'll pick you up in a little while," said Noelle.

"Good luck, secret santa and her trusty elf," Nick said, holding up the masks.

About an hour later Noelle picked up her niece and they headed toward downtown. Just as Noelle expected the shops were locked up tight and there was barely any traffic on the streets. She had Belle drive along the main street and turn to go around the back of the stores just to make sure no one was working late. They made all four sides behind the shops out of the cameras' views and Noelle was satisfied it was as safe as it was going to be.

She stepped out of the car and walked quickly to the big tree and dropped off the bag full of decorations. Then she kept walking to the opposite street from where Belle dropped her and waited behind a tree. She saw Belle approach and walked nonchalantly to the curb and got in the car.

Following the plan Belle drove them two blocks away and they started walking toward their goal. When they knew they would be in camera range they slid their masks on and secured the hoodies over their heads. Neither of them had said much since driving around the square; both were focused on the mission.

"Here we go," said Noelle as they walked up to the big tree where the bag was hidden. "Just like we practiced."

They walked the few steps to the small pine tree and dumped the contents of the bag next to it. Noelle grabbed the lights and began stringing them around the tree. Belle followed behind her hanging decorations here and there.

"I'm putting this one right in front," Belle whispered, showing Noelle one of the rainbow ornaments she'd purchased earlier with Sasha.

Noelle smiled, remembering the other ornament she'd hung on Sasha's tree when they got back from the square earlier that night.

"You get to put the star on this one," Noelle whispered, handing it to Belle.

She could see Belle's smile behind the elf mask she'd chosen earlier.

"Merry Christmas, Mimi," Belle whispered as she placed the star on the top branch of the pine.

They were both admiring their work when they saw lights coming down the street. "Shit," said Noelle in a loud whisper. "Get down!"

They both fell to the grass and flattened their bodies as much as they could. When the car passed them and kept going, they stayed down for a moment longer.

"Whew," said Noelle. "Let's go."

They hopped up, turned the lights on and hurriedly walked the other direction from where they'd entered the square. Once they were sure they were out of the range of the cameras they turned and walked back in the direction of the car.

"That one snuck up on us," commented Belle as they approached the car.

"I know," said Noelle. "We'll be more careful next time."

"The Great Christmas Tree Mystery has begun," Belle said merrily.

"I can't believe that's what everyone calls it," said Noelle, getting in the car.

"I like it." She grinned.

Noelle smiled and thought of her mother. *I'm trying to spread Christmas cheer just like you did, Mom.*

"Let's go to your place and celebrate with a drink," said Belle.

"Don't you have school tomorrow?"

"It's Friday. My juniors and seniors are presenting projects. I'll need this drink to get through those," she said, chuckling.

"Then let's go have that drink and choose our next tree," said Noelle.

6

The next day Sasha walked into the Santa Junction hardware store planning to pay for her tree and decorations and hoping to run into Noelle. She looked around for a moment and then went to the register and attempted to explain paying for things she didn't have in front of her.

"Hi," she said with a friendly smile. "I got a Christmas tree yesterday and had it delivered so I want to pay for it."

"No problem," the salesperson said. "Do you remember how big it was?"

"Oh, uh," she stammered.

"It was a six foot tree, Sam," Noelle said, walking up behind Sasha.

She whirled around and looked into those gorgeous green eyes and her heart skipped a beat. "Hey," she said, giving Noelle one of her best smiles. "I was hoping to run into you."

"Here I am," Noelle said, holding out her arms.

"Was there anything else?" Sam asked from behind the counter.

"Yes," Sasha said, turning back around. "There were two boxes of lights, and several ornaments."

"Not the tree, Sam," said Noelle. "I told you that was from me."

"Okay," said Sam, punching keys on the register.

"But..."

"No buts, I wanted to do it," Noelle said, smiling again.

"Well, thank you." Sasha handed Sam her money. "Keep the change. It's the least I can do."

"Thank you," said Sam, handing her the receipt.

Sasha moved out of the way of the next customer. "Are you working?"

"No."

Sasha looked at Noelle with a twinkle in her eye. "Did you hear that the Great Christmas Tree Mystery is back?"

"Oh," Noelle said, playing along. "I did hear something about a decorated Christmas tree."

"Rita was so excited when I came in this morning that she marched me out to the other side of the courthouse to show me. Have you seen it?"

"No. I heard about it though."

"Can I show you something?" asked Sasha, a hint of secrecy in her voice.

"Okay," Noelle said.

"You'll have to go with me," Sasha said, walking out of the store.

Noelle chuckled. "I think I can trust you."

They got into Sasha's car and drove towards her office on the west side of the square. "I wanted to show you the tree. I think there's something you'd recognize."

"Oh," said Noelle. "How is your tree?"

"You and that magical little tree have inspired me to unpack a few more boxes," said Sasha.

"Let me guess," said Noelle. "You haven't unpacked seasonal things and decided to look for your Christmas decorations?"

"Not exactly," Sasha said with a grin. "I haven't unpacked a lot of things, but I plan to unpack a few more things for the kitchen. Because I would like to cook dinner for us tomorrow night if that works for you." Sasha glanced over at Noelle to see her reaction.

"Tomorrow night would be great, but if you're cooking you have to let me bring something," Noelle said, smiling over at her.

"Hmm, let me see. You can bring a good crusty bread."

"Crusty bread. Okay, I can do that." Noelle nodded.

They entered the downtown square and Sasha parked right in front of the decorated tree.

"Isn't this sweet," Noelle said, looking the tree over.

"It is," commented Sasha.

"I have a clue for your investigation," Noelle said, looking around the tree at Sasha.

"What's that?"

"These lights," Noelle said, fingering the string, "are just like the ones at my brother's store." She widened her eyes playfully.

Sasha had to keep from grinning at her. "Come around here," she said. "Do you see anything that looks familiar?"

Noelle took a couple of steps around the small tree and looked at the ornaments. "Would you look at that? This tree has a rainbow covered in holly, too."

"Just like the one you got me last night," said Sasha.

"Is that another clue that the perpetrator shops locally or could even live among us?" Noelle teased.

Sasha chuckled. "I like to think my magical little tree wanted this one to share the Christmas spirit it gave us."

"This tree has certainly made me smile," said Noelle.

When they got back into the car, Noelle asked, "Who does Rita suspect? Hell, she probably knows."

"She has a few ideas, but isn't sure. All I know is she was elated this morning and said that the holiday season had officially started."

Noelle chuckled as she looked out the window.

"Come to think of it," Sasha said thoughtfully, "she said the same thing yesterday when you came into the office."

Noelle looked over at her and smiled. "I think this season just got a little merrier."

Sasha smiled back at her and thought that Noelle Winters had certainly made this Christmas take an interesting turn.

After a moment Noelle asked, "Are you seriously going to investigate this notorious tree decorator?"

"I don't know. It is a bit curious why they're doing it anonymously. That usually means someone has something to hide."

"But it does seem to spread Christmas cheer."

"It does. I think the whole town has been talking about it." She parked at the front of the hardware store and turned toward Noelle. "How about 6:00 tomorrow night?" Sasha asked.

"I'll be there with crusty bread," Noelle said with a smile. She opened the door and started to get out and then turned back to Sasha. "You know, I wouldn't mind helping you unpack boxes. That is, if you need help."

"I appreciate that," said Sasha. "I'll keep it in mind."

Noelle nodded. "I'll see you tomorrow." She got out and closed the door. She walked around the front of the car and came around to Sasha's window. She waited for Sasha to lower it and said, "I'm really glad I got to see you today."

"Me too," replied Sasha and with that Noelle walked into the store.

Sasha caught herself smiling as she drove back to the office thinking about Noelle Winters.

* * *

Noelle turned away from her small oven when she heard a knock on her door. "Come in," she called.

"What is that heavenly aroma?" Belle asked, walking inside and closing the door.

"I'm baking bread."

Belle took two steps to peer inside the oven window and then looked at her aunt. "Why are you feeling so domesticated this morning?" She only needed a few steps to land on the couch in Noelle's tiny house.

"I'm having dinner with Sasha tonight and she asked me to bring crusty bread. I thought it would be fun to surprise her by making it myself. I haven't done it in a long time, so if it isn't any good I can always buy a loaf on the way to her house."

"If it tastes as good as it smells you are going to get lucky tonight," said Belle.

"What?" Noelle said, chuckling.

"It's a date, isn't it?"

"Well, yeah."

"You obviously like her or you wouldn't be going."

"Yeah, but I'm not trying to get her in bed," said Noelle. However, sometimes when their eyes met she felt like she could melt into those soft brown eyes.

"Oh right. You're just making sure she doesn't find out that you're Santa's number one helper in charge of secretly decorating Christmas trees in our little town."

Noelle looked at her and smirked. "That's not why I'm going. I like her. She's interesting."

"And she's gorgeous!"

Noelle couldn't keep from smiling. "She is that."

"Uh huh, and available. Wouldn't it be nice to have a girlfriend here? Maybe you'd come home more often."

"You know, I was thinking I'd turn the Christmas tree decorating over to you," Noelle said, abruptly changing the subject.

"What? Why?"

"Because since Mom died it's hard to come home. I feel untethered. Most people would think that's freeing, but not for me. I need to feel like I have a place to land, a place that will always be there to hold me. It's hard to explain. I never imagined I'd feel this way," said Noelle. The honesty pouring out of her was a surprise, but also welcome because she'd finally put the feelings into words, at least somewhat.

"Aw, Aunt Noelle," said Belle. She got up and hugged her. "I think I understand what you mean."

"Don't get me wrong, I feel like I belong in our family, but it's just not the same. Something feels off," she said.

Belle nodded and sat back down. "Maybe Sasha is what you need then. Maybe she'll be a reason for you to come home. Here's an idea, maybe she could get you to stay!" she said animatedly. "Because you know, you could. There are plenty of people you could help around here."

"Wow, that's kind of fast, isn't it?"

"Not really. Come on Aunt Noelle, when's the last time you went on a date when you came home for Christmas?" Before she could say anything Belle continued. "When's the last time you went on a date, period?"

Noelle didn't answer her. Belle had a point. She hadn't been on a date in ages and she was looking forward to dinner tonight with Sasha. The timer dinged and she went back to the oven to check the bread.

"I know the answer," said Belle, watching her aunt take the bread out of the oven. "You may not have admitted it to yourself, dear Auntie, but you like Sasha Solomon or you wouldn't be baking bread, hoping to impress her tonight."

Noelle looked at her as she set the rounded loaf on the stove.

"Would you do something for me?" asked Belle.

"What?"

"Would you let go of all the tragedy and sadness that I know you see everyday in your job and let this holiday wrap you in comfort? Let Santa Junction, let the trees, let Sasha hold on to you for just a little while and take in some of that joy brought to this town from decorating these trees," said Belle with love in her eyes.

Noelle stared at her niece and considered her words. She thought of her job as helping people get back on their feet, but she did see much sadness and sometimes it was hard to let that go. That's one reason that when she looked into Sasha's eyes she saw a confidant of sorts—she knew Sasha had seen the same things.

She smiled at Belle. "Do you think this bread will impress her?

Belle gave her a knowing smile. "Oh yeah."

"I heard what you said, Belle."

"Good. Now what are you going to wear?" she said, walking past her aunt and into her bedroom.

7

Sasha opened the door to a smiling Noelle. "Hi, come in," she said, stepping aside so Noelle could enter.

"Thanks," Noelle said, walking in and turning towards Sasha. "We were kind of busy the other night but I meant to tell you how lovely your home is."

"Thank you. I'll give you a tour," she said. Then she noticed the bag in Noelle's hands. "Let's go in the kitchen so you can set that down."

Noelle followed her into the kitchen and set the bag on the counter. She reached inside and pulled out a bottle of wine. "I brought this," she said, handing it to Sasha.

"Oh, I should have told you, I don't drink," she said, holding the bottle. She looked into those gentle green eyes. "You know, I find it so easy to be honest with you." She took a breath and continued. "A few years ago I realized that instead of dealing with some of the feelings that go along with my job, especially when in a tragic situation, I was pushing them down with alcohol. I decided it would be much healthier to stop drinking."

"I understand exactly what you're saying. I'm not a big

drinker myself." Noelle took the bottle from Sasha and set it on the counter. "Why don't we find someone else who can enjoy this?"

"I don't want you to not drink because of me," said Sasha.

"I'm not." Noelle leaned in and said, "Honestly, I thought you were supposed to bring wine when someone was cooking for you."

Sasha chuckled. "I know. Who made that rule?" she said playfully. "You're sure?"

"I'm sure."

Sasha nodded and their eyes locked. *How adorable was this woman?* She found herself wanting to know all about Noelle Winters.

Noelle pulled her stare away and reached back into the bag. She took out the loaf of bread wrapped in a towel.

"What's this?" Sasha exclaimed. "Homemade bread!"

"I haven't made it in a long time so I hope it's good," Noelle said tentatively.

Sasha unwrapped the bread and took a deep breath. "It smells divine." She opened a drawer and took out a bread knife and sliced off the heel. Then she sliced another small piece and picked it up. "I love the heel." She took a small bite and moaned.

"It's okay? I didn't want to cut it before I got here," said Noelle.

Sasha cut off a bite sized piece and held it to Noelle's mouth.

She opened her mouth and tasted the bread, her gaze never leaving Sasha's. "It's good," she said.

"Good? It's delicious," said Sasha. "I am so impressed!"

Noelle laughed. "My niece said you would be."

Sasha tilted her head. "Did you want to impress me?"

Noelle raised her eyebrows. "I guess I did." Then she gave her a sweet smile and sniffed. "But what is that wonderful smell, because it's not this bread?"

"I made soup. I thought a cozy cold evening called for soup and crusty bread," Sasha said, walking to a large pot on the stove, removing the lid and stirring the contents.

"I couldn't agree more. It smells wonderful," said Noelle.

Sasha returned the lid to the pot. "Time for the house tour." She held out her arms. "This is the kitchen."

"It's beautiful. I love the white cabinets."

"That's what sold me on the house. I love the farmhouse look and I enjoy cooking, but haven't done much since moving here," she explained.

"It must be that unpacking issue you told me about because it can't be the wide variety of restaurants in our little town," said Noelle.

"The restaurants here are fine. Well, the ones I've tried. I don't really like eating alone in a restaurant so I've become quite the take-out queen," she explained.

"I'm the same way. How about since you're cooking for me, I'll take you to the restaurant of your choice in Santa Junction?"

Sasha smiled and considered Noelle's offer. "I'd like that. You are brightening this holiday for me, Noelle Winters."

"I'm glad, but were you not looking forward to it?"

"Holidays can be hard."

Noelle nodded her understanding.

"Let me show you the rest of the house," said Sasha. Noelle followed her into the living room and down a hallway. "This room on the left is my office," she said, walking in and turning the light on.

"Oh, this is nice," said Noelle. "I'm not surprised."

"What do you mean?"

"It's all neat and tidy. I thought you would be organized," said Noelle.

"Hmm," said Sasha, raising her eyebrows and realizing that meant Noelle had been thinking about her too. "You may rethink that when you see the room across the hall that will eventually become the guest room."

Noelle peeked inside the room and saw stacks of boxes on one wall. There was a bed and a dresser scooted to the other side of the room. "It looks like a guest room now," she said kindly. "I mean someone could sleep there, right?"

Sasha chuckled. "I guess they could, but you're seeing what I still need to unpack. That doesn't count the things I have in storage in the city."

"If you need help..." said Noelle. "Or are you putting it off?"

Sasha met Noelle's eyes. "At first, maybe I was apprehensive I'd actually do this. But now I know I'm staying."

"Then let me help you at least find your Christmas decorations. Your magical little tree wouldn't want to be all alone."

"Okay," said Sasha. "We can start on them after dinner. You weren't expecting me to be so much fun on a first date, were you?"

Noelle reached out and put her hand on Sasha's arm. "I can't think of a better way to get to know you than to unload your treasures."

"My treasures?" Sasha said, searching Noelle's eyes. "There might be a few."

She turned and showed Noelle a bathroom further down the hall and then the master bedroom.

Noelle walked into the large room and Sasha watched her eye the bed. It was an exquisite four-poster piece of craftsmanship with an ornate design on the headboard. Spread over it was a beautiful quilt that looked handmade.

"This is incredible. It's beautiful," Noelle whispered, gently running her hand over the fabric. "It certainly completes your farmhouse charm."

"It was an indulgence when I moved here. I feel like I have a farmhouse, just not the farm."

"My whole house would almost fit in this room," said Noelle, gazing around the rest of the room and poking her head in the master bath.

"What do you mean?"

"When my mom died, Nick and I decided to sell our family home. He wanted me to have my own place when I came home to visit so we built a tiny house on the back of his property."

"I love to watch those shows about tiny houses!" exclaimed Sasha.

Noelle laughed. "Yeah well, a tiny house is okay for a little while, but I wouldn't want to live in it year round."

"Can I see it? I'm really curious," said Sasha.

"Of course you can. How about tomorrow?"

Sasha nodded. "I'd like that." Her stomach chose that particular moment to rumble loudly and her eyes went wide, but with Noelle she didn't feel self-conscious at all. She felt comfortable. "I think it's time to eat."

Noelle chuckled. "We've resisted these tempting aromas long enough."

They went back into the kitchen and Sasha dished them each a big bowl of warm soup while Noelle cut the bread into slices. She found butter in the refrigerator and they ate at the table in the kitchen.

They talked of where their jobs had led them around the world. And sure enough, Noelle had followed behind Sasha in several of the places she'd reported from. They discovered they had stayed in the same hotel at three different locations, but had not run into one another.

"This is nice," Noelle said, leaning back from the table. She looked over at Sasha and studied her for a moment.

"What's that look?" said Sasha softly.

"I was just thinking that I wish we would have run into each other."

"Do you?" asked Sasha. "I found it hard to make a lasting connection under those circumstances, if you know what I mean."

"If you mean all those intense emotions that were magnified and had to go somewhere—I think I know where they would've gone between us."

Sasha could feel the heat building in her cheeks and Noelle's eyes turned a dark emerald green. "When you see that much heartache and despair you want to feel alive."

Noelle exhaled. "That was another way to bury feelings or would it be to express them?"

"You know as well as I do that it was easy to fall into bed with a like-minded warm body when it became too much."

Noelle smiled. "There is absolutely no judgement here. I had my fair share of 'expressing those feelings,'" she said, using her hands to make air quotes. "But I grew to hate the emptiness that followed and while you chose not to drink any longer, I stopped jumping into bed."

"Then I'm glad we met under *these* circumstances."

Noelle tilted her head with an uncertain look on her face. "Because?"

"Because I hope there's more to us than that," Sasha said boldly. She noticed Noelle's chest begin to rise and fall faster.

"What did Rita have to say about our date?" said Noelle.

Sasha smirked. "Are you changing the subject?"

"Not at all. I would think she is our biggest fan," said Noelle with a smile.

"I knew she would be talking about it all day so I didn't tell her I was having you over for dinner until almost quitting time." Sasha grinned. "To say she was giddy would be an understatement."

Noelle laughed.

"She really likes you. So much so that she wants you to move back here," said Sasha.

"Oh, I'm aware. She comes up with a different reason for me to stay every holiday. I think my mom must have asked her to keep an eye on me as a favor and she took it to heart."

"It's really very sweet."

"I know, but sometimes..."

Sasha's phone began to ring and she looked at Noelle. "I should get that because of the paper and all," she stammered.

"Of course, go ahead."

When Sasha came back into the kitchen she said, "Are you up for a little adventure?"

"Sure," answered Noelle excitedly.

"There has been a report of someone decorating a Christmas tree. Shall we go see?"

Noelle jumped up and followed Sasha to her car.

8

They got in Sasha's car and she backed out of the driveway.

"Where are we going?" asked Noelle. She was amused because she and Belle had been planning another tree decorating caper for later that night. But now she wondered if there was a copycat decorator in their midst.

"Settler's Park. Apparently Rita set up some kind of tip line on the website. My copy editor was updating a story and noticed the tip so he called me," she explained.

"A tip line!" exclaimed Noelle. "She's serious about finding the person, isn't she?"

"As much as I've come to adore Rita in the short time I've been here, she is a little nosy," said Sasha affectionately.

"A little!" exclaimed Noelle, laughing.

Sasha chuckled. "That's why she's good at her job."

She steered the car into the entrance of the park and took the road to the right.

"Did they say where in the park?" asked Noelle, looking out her window as they slowly drove by the large pond.

"No, just in the park," said Sasha. She peered out her

window and then saw car lights ahead. They met another car that was driving through from the other entrance.

"Do you think it was them?" Noelle asked excitedly.

Sasha looked over at her. "Are you teasing me?"

Noelle's face fell. Then she smiled and said, "Maybe a little."

Sasha laughed. "Come on, don't you want to know who is doing it?"

"Not really. I think there's a reason they don't want to be found out."

"Maybe, but it still makes me wonder."

"Those investigator instincts don't fade away in a small town," commented Noelle.

"Never. I'm naturally curious," replied Sasha. "However, I'm not actively looking to investigate as I once did. I enjoy writing stories for the paper and am putting ideas together for a book."

"You are? It will be a bestseller," said Noelle.

"What? Why would you say that?"

"Because I know where you've been and you're a compassionate person. It will be a hit."

"How do you know I'm compassionate?"

"Because I watched your reports. Your audience can see how dedicated you are to the people you're covering," she said. "It came through on camera. Without fangirling, I respect the stories you chose to tell and not exploit the situations."

Sasha looked over at her with a warm smile. "Thank you."

Noelle smiled and when Sasha looked back to the road she said, "You are also a beautiful, smart, talented journalist that just happens to be a lesbian, so I couldn't keep from watching your reports when TV was available where I was working."

"Oh, so was it my journalistic talent or the fact that I'm a lesbian?" Sasha asked with a smirk.

"Will it make it awkward if I admit that I might have had a little crush on you?" said Noelle.

Sasha pulled over and looked at Noelle. "Really?"

Noelle nodded. "I don't think there is anyone in the park decorating trees, but I do think it's a nice night for a walk in the moonlight."

They had only seen the one car since entering the park. Sasha turned off the engine and said to Noelle, "I'd like that."

They both got out of the car and Noelle said, "Let's go this way." She reached out her hand to Sasha and she took it. Noelle intertwined their fingers and her heart skipped a beat. She couldn't remember the last time she'd held a woman's hand. But this wasn't any woman; this was Sasha Solomon. She took a deep breath, trying to calm her beating heart and took that moment to relish the feel of Sasha's soft, warm hand in hers.

They walked along in comfortable silence for a few moments. "I think you may have gotten a bad tip," suggested Noelle.

"Maybe," replied Sasha, squeezing Noelle's hand. "But I get to walk in the moonlight with a romantic woman."

"Romantic, huh." Noelle glanced sideways at Sasha as they continued to stroll around the pond.

"Yes. You did bring me homemade bread when you know I love to cook and then you jumped in the car and came along on this wild goose chase."

"But I'm on a romantic walk in the moonlight with an incredibly beautiful woman," Noelle said. "However, we are not coming any closer to finding your packed away Christmas decorations."

"True. What about tomorrow?"

"Well..." Noelle said dramatically, "this interesting journalist is coming over tomorrow to see my tiny house. And believe me, when she sees my tiny kitchen she's going to be even more impressed that bread came from it."

Sasha chuckled. "I can't wait."

Noelle stopped and turned towards Sasha. "Look up," she said to the slightly taller woman.

Sasha complied."What?"

Noelle got her phone out of her pocket and turned on the flashlight, then pointed it above them.

Sasha grinned. "Mistletoe!" she exclaimed.

Noelle put her phone back in her pocket and gently placed her hand on the side of Sasha's face. She saw the smile fade and Sasha's eyes darken. *My God this woman is sexy*, Noelle thought. She slowly leaned in and felt Sasha's hands settle on her hips as she closed the distance between their lips. When her lips touched Sasha's full, supple mouth it was better than she had imagined. It was as if their lips were made for one another. Sasha's hands roamed up her back and pulled her closer. When their lips parted with a gentle smack Noelle felt weak in the knees.

Sasha was staring into her eyes with such a sultry look. Before Noelle could do anything but breathe Sasha brought their lips together again. This time she felt Sasha's teeth nibble at her bottom lip and her heart pounded in her chest. Her arms were around Sasha's shoulders now, holding on, and she deepened the kiss. As if in perfect harmony their lips parted slightly and their tongues met in a soft sensual touch that sent a zap of electricity down to Noelle's core.

This woman had woken up a part of Noelle that had

been dormant for way too long. She heard and felt the moan escape her throat and slip past her lips. Sasha's arms held her tighter. For several moments their tongues explored and their lips caressed one another's. The kiss finally came to an end and they pulled back slightly.

Noelle smiled shyly and took Sasha's hand and pulled them toward the trees. She stopped and reached up into one of the lower branches and snapped a small piece of mistletoe from the bundle. With a smile she handed it to Sasha. "For you. We should hang it on your tree."

Sasha returned her smile and nodded. "I don't have to have a piece of mistletoe every time I want to kiss you, do I?"

Noelle chuckled and shook her head.

"Because if I do, then I'm carrying a piece around in my coat pocket," Sasha added with her eyebrows raised.

Noelle leaned in and gave Sasha a sweet soft kiss. "You can kiss me anytime you want."

"Mmm," Sasha said, looking into Noelle's eyes and studying her face. She ran her finger along Noelle's cheek and rubbed her thumb over her bottom lip. "Such beautiful lips," she whispered, gently placing hers on Noelle's.

This time they both leaned back and Sasha took Noelle's hand. They began the walk back to the car. "Shall I text you tomorrow before I come to your house?"

"I admit that I like to sleep in on weekends, but..."

Sasha chuckled. "Don't worry, it won't be until afternoon."

They got back to the car and Sasha walked them to the passenger side. She took a lock of Noelle's hair and curled it behind her ear. "You are so beautiful. Those green eyes are bewitching."

Noelle smiled as Sasha touched her lips to hers again in

a slow sweet kiss. Their foreheads met and Noelle said breathlessly, "Your kisses are enchanting."

Sasha opened the door and once Noelle was inside she went around to the driver's side. They looked out at the trees as they made one more drive through the park.

"Let me know when you get another tip. I'll go with you," said Noelle, rubbing Sasha's shoulder.

"I didn't think you cared who was doing it."

"I don't, but I sure like helping you look."

Sasha laughed and drove them to her house.

9

When they returned to Sasha's house Noelle went inside and helped her hang the mistletoe. They shared more delicious kisses and Noelle didn't want to leave, but she knew Belle was waiting for her. She couldn't wait for tomorrow when she'd get to see Sasha again.

"Hey," Belle said, getting in her car. "You must have had a wonderful time because you're late."

Noelle couldn't hide her smile even in the dark car. "I had an amazing time."

Belle chuckled. "You're kind of glowing over there, Auntie."

Noelle didn't say anything but the smile never left her face.

"I can't believe you went to the park looking for, well... us?"

"I told you someone gave them a tip. For a minute there I did wonder if someone else was decorating trees. How ironic that the park is our next target."

"Oh, do you think there's something magical going on?" Belle said in a mysterious voice.

"No. We saw one car and that was it."

"I'm not going to ask you why you were late then."

Noelle chuckled. She pulled the car into the park and drove down a short dirt road. Then she steered it under a tree so if someone happened to drive through they wouldn't see the car. They got the bag out of the back and hiked through the trees to the other side of the park. The tree they planned to decorate was just ahead. They dropped the bag and began to get the lights and decorations out when they saw lights coming their way.

"Shit," said Noelle. "Drop the stuff and hide!"

They ran back into the woods and crouched down behind a cluster of trees out of sight. Noelle watched as the car pulled over not too far from the tree they planned to decorate.

"What now?" whispered Belle.

"We wait."

"Please tell me that isn't a couple of kids about to get busy on a Saturday night," Belle whispered loudly.

Noelle chuckled.

"What's so funny?"

"Calling them kids is kind of rich coming from you since you're all of twenty-four."

"Do you think they can hear us?"

"No, their windows are up."

"Well, tell me about your date then."

"She said I was romantic," Noelle said, thinking back to the kisses they shared not too far from where she and Belle were huddled.

"You are."

"I could still be over at her house," said Noelle.

"Then why aren't you? We could do this any night."

Noelle sighed.

"Let me guess. She's not like the other women you've told me about from time to time in your job. You like her."

"I didn't *not* like the others," protested Noelle.

"I know that. This is different. You knew with the others that it was a short term thing. This isn't."

"I don't know what this is. That's the problem."

"Well, let your favorite niece clear it up for you," said Belle. "I can tell you like her. What happens if this goes somewhere? I know what you're going to say. 'I'm leaving.' But what if you didn't?"

"What?"

"What if you stayed? I know it's hard without Mimi, Noelle. But have you considered the idea of coming home and living in her memory? The sadness would fade and all the good memories are what you'd see every day. You wouldn't be alone; Sasha is here."

"Are these people ever going to leave? I'm getting cold," said Noelle.

"Do you really want to give up a chance with a woman like Sasha Solomon because you're afraid? She likes you Noelle."

"How do you know that?"

"Because she's a smart woman and there's no way a woman like that is going to let you get away without finding out what's in your heart."

"What makes you think I can just quit my job?"

"I saw the tiredness in your eyes when you got home and after you met Sasha Solomon the twinkle came back. That twinkle has nothing to do with these trees; it's all her."

Noelle considered her niece's words. She was tired and knew when she'd left New York City it was doubtful she'd be back, but Santa Junction was the last place she expected to stay.

"You don't have to decide it all tonight," said Belle. "Spend the holiday with Sasha, decorate trees, and let the Christmas magic go to work."

Noelle looked over at Belle. "Sasha claims her Christmas tree is magical and we happened across some mistletoe while we were out here earlier."

"I hope you took some to her place," said Belle in a loud whisper.

"We did. She's coming over tomorrow to see the tiny house."

"Please let her in your heart," pleaded Belle.

Noelle smiled at her. "She's already there," she said quietly.

"Do not push her away!"

"Shhh," said Noelle. "I couldn't even if I wanted to, Belle. Not after she kissed me tonight."

Belle grinned. "This is going to be a great Christmas."

Noelle couldn't help but smile.

"Look!" exclaimed Belle. "They're leaving. Finally!"

They watched the car drive away and when Belle started to get up Noelle said, "Wait. Let's give it a couple of minutes."

Belle crouched back down and waited.

"Thanks, Belle. I'm lucky to have such a smart niece."

"You are," she teased. "Come on, let's get this done."

They made it back to the tree and made quick work of getting the lights on. They were hanging the decorations when Belle said, "Can you help me open this one? Next time let's open all the boxes and then put them in the bag. I can't get this plastic off."

"Here, I'll open it," Noelle said, taking her gloves off. She opened the package and handed the ornament to Belle. Then she reached in the bag for the rainbow ornament with the holly on top. She planned to put this ornament on all these trees this year. Once again, she hung it right in the front and imagined the delighted smile on Sasha's face when she saw it.

Belle gathered up the trash and said, "Here are your gloves."

"Throw them in the bag. I'll get them when we get home." Noelle straightened the star on the top branch. "Ready?" she asked before turning the lights on.

"Ready."

Noelle flipped the switch and they gazed at the tree. "This has been such a good night," she said as they hurried back to the car. They got in and kept their lights off as they went out the other entrance. Once they were on the street, Noelle turned the lights on and drove them home.

After she dropped Belle off she grabbed the bags out of the back seat and took them inside. She'd throw the trash away in the morning and go through her stock of decorations to see what she needed to replenish.

She fell asleep thinking about the kisses under the mistletoe and looking forward to tomorrow.

10

The next day Noelle tidied her house which didn't take much. Having lived in a tiny house for a while, she'd learned that everything has a place and once she used something she put it back. She had learned quickly that there was no room for clutter. She was looking through her supply of ornaments and emptying the trash from last night when her phone pinged.

A smile immediately grew on her face as she read the text and quickly looked around the living/kitchen area. She stuffed the bag of decorating trash in the bottom cubby of the open cabinet and went out the door.

There was Sasha standing next to her car. Her face lit up when she saw Noelle. She waved her over and walked across the yard to meet her.

"I hope I'm not too eager," Sasha said, scrunching up her face.

"Are you eager?" Noelle asked, tilting her head and grinning.

"What do you think?" She leaned in and kissed Noelle softly on the lips.

"Come on in," Noelle said, grabbing her hand.

"This is lovely back here." Sasha gazed over the yard. "All the trees."

"It's kind of secluded, until you look over there," Noelle said, gesturing towards the back of her brother's house. Lisa was looking out the kitchen window and Noelle chuckled and waved.

Sasha waved at her too. "I forgot Lisa was your sister-in-law. She was one of the first people I met here. I should get her to partner with me on this investigation. I've heard she's a brilliant detective."

Noelle suddenly started coughing and Sasha rubbed her back. "Are you all right?"

"Yes," she said. "It must be allergies." She led them towards the door and opened it. "After you."

* * *

Sasha walked into the tiny house and looked to her right, left, and then spun around. "Oh Noelle, it's gorgeous!" she exclaimed.

Noelle followed her in. "Let me show you around." She held her arms out wide and swept them around. "If you look this way, you'll find the living room and a few feet to your right and you'll be in the kitchen." She chuckled.

"I love it," Sasha said, walking in the living area and looking out the window. On one wall was a couch and across from it was a small TV surrounded by bookshelves with storage underneath. There were high windows near the ceiling to bring in more light. She looked back through the room to the kitchen area and noticed something on the floor.

"Here's the kitchen," said Noelle.

Sasha took the few steps then bent down and picked something up. "Did you lose this?" She handed Noelle a glove that looked familiar.

"Oh, the other one is around here somewhere. Thanks," she said, taking the glove and putting it on the counter.

Sasha bent back down and looked around for the other glove. "I don't see it," she said, standing back up. "But you have plenty of Christmas decorations in there." Sasha looked around and then back at Noelle. "You haven't put them up yet. Do you want help?" she offered.

"No," said Noelle quickly. "Our mission today is to find yours."

Sasha nodded. "Then your house is next."

"Agreed," Noelle stated. "Let me show you the bathroom and bedroom. This way."

"Wait!" said Sasha. "You haven't let me look at this beautifully efficient kitchen and be impressed with your baking skills."

"Please," said Noelle, chuckling. "Take your time. I aim to impress."

Sasha gazed at her with a smirk. "Oh, I'm impressed all right."

Noelle grinned and stopped outside the bathroom. She moved so Sasha could look inside and then she walked in and spun around. "This is surprisingly spacious. What a smart use of space." She stood in the doorway and was almost chest to chest with Noelle.

"I almost forgot," she said, gazing into Noelle's eyes. "I brought you something." She reached in her pocket and pulled out a sprig of mistletoe, dangling it between them. Then she held it over Noelle's head and looked back into her eyes.

She softly laid her lips on Noelle's and her stomach

flipped. God, this woman's lips were pillow-soft and felt exquisite against hers. She didn't want to pull away, but she did slowly and lowered the mistletoe.

"I went to the park to get a sprig of mistletoe for you. I mean after all I couldn't come to your house without bringing something, right?"

"All you have to bring are these lips," Noelle said, kissing her again.

"You'll never believe what I saw at the park," said Sasha, rubbing her lips together.

"Uh, a tree?" Noelle asked playfully.

Sasha giggled. "I did see a few of those, but I also saw a decorated Christmas tree."

"What?" Noelle raised her brows.

"Maybe that tip was a little premature last night because there is definitely a decorated tree in the park today."

"Hmm," Noelle said. "What do you make of that?"

"I don't know. It's interesting, but," she paused. "Not as interesting as this." Sasha slowly leaned in and put her lips on Noelle's for another kiss. This one made her weak in the knees.

Noelle took a breath and said, "Here's the bedroom."

Sasha took a deep breath of her own and gathered herself, knowing she wasn't the only one affected by that kiss. She took a step through the doorway and before she spoke Noelle said, "It's certainly not as extravagant as yours."

"But I love it just the same," said Sasha. "It's so cozy." She looked over at Noelle. "I think we should try them both."

Noelle raised her eyebrows.

"Is that too bold? Have you not thought about it?"

Noelle gave her a slow sexy smile and put her hands on

Sasha's shoulders. She gently pushed them to sit on the bed and then pulled her closer. Their lips met and she quickly deepened the kiss.

They fell over and Sasha loved the feel of Noelle on top of her. Their kisses were hot and wet and oh so good. Sasha immediately missed Noelle's lips when she pulled away.

"Of course I've thought about it," said Noelle, breathing hard.

Sasha still had the mistletoe in her fingers and raised it over Noelle's head and dangled it. She raised her eyebrows and Noelle's response was to claim Sasha's lips in another heated kiss.

"Mmm," Sasha moaned. "Your lips were made for mine," she whispered.

Noelle looked into her eyes and smiled. She ran her thumb along her cheek.

Sasha stroked Noelle's hair. "You have the most beautiful deep auburn hair. I imagine that's what the fire looks like that you light inside me with those kisses." She shook her head. "Sorry, you've done something to me."

"I hope it's a good something," Noelle said softly.

"Oh, believe me, it is," said Sasha. *Those green eyes are mesmerizing, she thought*. She pulled Noelle down into another scorching kiss. After several moments Sasha was thinking maybe it was time to lose their clothes when they heard a knock at the door.

Noelle pulled away. "Maybe they'll go away," she teased.

Sasha laughed and pushed her up. "They know we're in here."

Noelle kissed her again quickly and hopped up. She gave Sasha her hand and pulled her up and then went to the door.

Sasha smoothed her hair down and walked into the kitchen.

"Hi Sasha," said Lisa. "I was just asking Noelle if you two would like to join us for Sunday lunch?"

Sasha looked at Noelle with a twinkle in her eye. "That would be lovely. Can I help?"

Lisa walked out the door with Sasha following behind her. She stopped and patted Noelle's cheek and winked at her.

Sasha enjoyed watching Noelle interact with her family during lunch. Their playful banter made it obvious how happy they were that she was home. Both Nick and Lisa included her in the conversation and when Nick started to tell stories about Noelle she said, "Oops, it's time for us to go."

Nick laughed. "Oh come on, it's a really good story."

Noelle stared at him and Lisa intervened. "How is Rita?" she asked Sasha.

"Rita is one of the most entertaining co-workers I've ever had," Sasha said with a genuine smile.

"Oh, I'm sure that's true," said Lisa.

"She is actually very happy with us both," Sasha said, looking over at Noelle. "I think we have given her a Christmas gift by going on a date."

"When you tell her there's been more than one she may explode with joy," teased Noelle.

They laughed and Sasha said, "I almost forgot. Rita has set up a tip line on the website. She is determined for me to solve The Great Christmas Tree Mystery. I told Noelle that I should enlist your detective skills to help me."

Lisa looked from Sasha to Noelle. "Hmm, that might be an interesting case."

"Wonder why she wants to find out so bad?" asked Nick.

"Like I told Noelle, one reason is because she's nosy," Sasha said, chuckling. "But she wants to give the person or persons a proper thank you."

"Oh, that's nice," said Lisa.

"Yeah, but they must not want to be thanked or they wouldn't stay anonymous," said Nick.

"True, but it does make me wonder why they do it. I mean, there has to be a reason. I wonder if they realize just how much Christmas cheer they're spreading because people are talking about it all over town."

"Give me a call tomorrow and let's look into it," said Lisa.

Sasha nodded.

"We have our own investigation today," said Noelle. "We are searching for Sasha's Christmas decorations that are packed away. Shall we get to it?"

Sasha smiled at Noelle. As much as she was enjoying herself she looked forward to having Noelle all to herself. She turned to Lisa and Nick. "Thank you so much for lunch. Can we help clean up?"

"No ma'am. That's Nick's job," said Lisa.

"It is," he said, getting up.

"This has been so nice," said Sasha.

"Yeah, thanks. It was fun," said Noelle.

"We're glad you both joined us."

They walked back to Noelle's and Sasha said, "They are really nice."

"Yeah they are. I'll be right back," Noelle said, walking into the bedroom.

Sasha sat on the couch and gazed around the room. Her eyes landed on that bottom storage area with all the Christmas decorations. What was it about that glove that reminded her of something? Maybe she'd seen Noelle wear it. That must be it.

Noelle walked back into the room and all Sasha could see were those gorgeous green eyes locked on hers. She wanted more than kisses from this woman.

11

Noelle followed Sasha to her house. She couldn't believe Sasha had gone back to the park for mistletoe and discovered the decorated tree. Luckily Sasha hadn't noticed that Noelle's coughing fit had been brought on by her surprise. Lisa had handled Sasha's invitation to help with the investigation like the police professional she was. But Noelle still needed to do something with all those decorations before Sasha came back to her place and wanted to put them up. That glove almost got her caught; she'd look for the other one when she got back home. It was probably stuck in the sack.

Deep down she wouldn't mind if Sasha found out she decorated the trees. She just didn't want the rest of the town to know. That would end it for her. The idea was to anonymously spread Christmas cheer just like her mom had. Noelle sighed loudly.

"Stop thinking about it," she said quietly. "All I want to think about is spending the day with Sasha Solomon." When she had come out of her bedroom earlier, the heated look Sasha gave her immediately had her cheeks turning red. She felt sure there would have been more than kisses shared on her bed if Lisa hadn't knocked on her door.

After parking, Noelle followed Sasha up to her front door and smiled when she turned and faced her.

"I think I left the mistletoe on your bed," Sasha said.

"I'll hang it over the bed when I get home. It will be waiting on you," said Noelle. Sasha stared into Noelle's eyes and she could feel her heart start to speed up. Sasha visibly exhaled and turned to unlock the door.

"I'm finding it hard to concentrate when you look at me with those sparkling green eyes. I think they are full of Christmas mischief," Sasha said, opening the door and walking inside.

"I don't think it's mischief." Noelle grabbed Sasha's hand and spun her around. She put her hands on Sasha's hips and pulled her close.

Sasha squealed with surprise and put her arms around Noelle's shoulders. She gazed into Noelle's eyes. "Hmm, what is it I see?"

A sexy smile spread over Noelle's face as she held Sasha tight. "Let's find those decorations."

Sasha brought her hand to Noelle's cheek and ran her thumb along it. "Okay," she whispered and leaned in for a slow, soft kiss. She pulled away and walked toward the hall as she took her coat off and dropped it on a chair.

"Fuck," Noelle said softly, drawing the word out. She took her coat off and threw it on top of Sasha's then followed her down the hall and into the guest room.

"Did you say something?" Sasha asked innocently, standing in front of a stack of boxes.

"You heard me," Noelle said with a smirk, walking over to another stack of boxes. "So do we just start opening and looking?"

"I guess so. I know the boxes on this end are knick knacks from growing up."

"Where *did* you grow up?"

"Everywhere," she said heavily. "Unlike you I don't have roots. My dad worked for a large multinational corporation and we relocated a lot. He would go into a location that wasn't doing well and help put them back on track. Sometimes that took a year, sometimes longer. That's how I found my love of cooking."

"What do you mean?"

"I spent a lot of time in the kitchen with my mom instead of out with friends."

"You didn't have friends?"

"Not really. I went to two different middle schools and three different high schools, all in different countries." Sasha shrugged.

"Oh my gosh!"

"Yeah. Growing up that way made it seem natural to go into journalism and work all over the world. College was probably the longest I stayed in one place since elementary school."

"That is so different from the way I grew up. My family has been in this town since forever," said Noelle.

"I think I was drawn to a smaller town because I wanted to see what it was like. We lived in some smaller cities, but they were still cities."

"What do you want to experience about small town living? I'd be glad to show you," Noelle said with a compassionate look.

Sasha stopped and stared at Noelle for a moment. "It was nice seeing people I'd met say hello to me on the sidewalk last night. What about you? While I grew up all over and am now gravitating toward a small town, you grew up here, but haven't moved back."

"I've stayed in my job longer than most people do. They get tired of traveling or moving from one catastrophe to the next. I think I'm afraid to assess why I haven't left yet, but it's probably because I don't know where to go."

"You don't want to come home?"

The way Sasha said that made Noelle's heart ache for her. She could tell in her voice that she longed for what she thought Noelle had. "For a long time I thought that I would eventually come back here, but after my mom died that changed. It's hard to explain."

Sasha walked over and put her hand on Noelle's shoulder. "I'm so sorry, Noelle."

"There you go with that compassion in your voice," Noelle said, trying to lighten the conversation.

"It's because I care and wish I could make it better."

"But why? We haven't known each other long."

Sasha smiled and gazed into Noelle's eyes. "I want to know you, Noelle. Rita may have introduced us, but the minute you walked into the newspaper office I wanted to know more."

"Did I hide how starstruck I was that day? Did you notice I held on to your hand a little too long?"

"I thought it was me holding onto yours." She smiled.

"You have given me more happiness in the last few days than I've felt in the last three Christmases here," Noelle said with a smile. "Is Christmases even a word? You're the journalist."

Sasha chuckled. "What a nice thing to say and yes Christmases is a word."

Noelle looked down at the box she had been opening and exclaimed, "Look!"

Sasha looked inside. "You found them!" She hugged Noelle tightly and when she let go they both stopped with their arms still loosely around each other. "Let's get these decorations put up because there's something else I want to do."

"What's that?" asked Noelle.

"I plan to take up where we left off before your sister-in-law knocked on your door."

Noelle gave her a knowing smile, widened her eyes and grabbed the box. "Let's go."

Sasha laughed and followed her into the living room. They made quick work unloading the box.

As Sasha hung the ornaments, she told Noelle the stories behind them. "I forgot to tell you. Guess what ornament was on the tree in the park?"

Noelle gazed at the rainbow with holly on it that she'd bought for Sasha's tree. "Not another rainbow?" she guessed, knowing full well it was there because she'd hung it herself the previous night.

"Yep. I like our mysterious elf's style," she said, hanging the last ornament.

They stepped back and admired the tree.

"This doesn't look like the same tree you delivered," said Sasha. "It gets more beautiful every day."

"It really does look good. I knew it would look better with ornaments on it, but I never dreamed it would fill out like this."

"It's Christmas magic," she said, putting her arm around Noelle.

She rested her head on Sasha's shoulder and exhaled. For the first time since losing her mom she felt a moment of peace and contentment in Santa Junction. Maybe it wasn't a magical tree. Maybe Sasha Solomon was the magic.

They found another box of Christmas knick knacks and a few Christmas dishes that they put in the dishwasher.

"Since you're the baker, maybe you could fill these plates with Christmas treats," Sasha said playfully.

Noelle chuckled. "I'll see what I can do. Are there any more decorations?"

"That's all that I want to put up inside. Maybe you could help me put up outdoor lights?" she asked with a hopeful look.

Those big brown eyes swaddled her like a warm blanket and she was pulled into Sasha's arms. "You can have whatever you want if you keep looking at me that way," Noelle said breathlessly.

"Mmm." Sasha moaned deep in her throat. "I know what I want." She took Noelle's lips with her own and began a slow, sensual assault with her mouth. She caressed her with her lips and bathed her in passion with her tongue.

Noelle's heart was about to beat out of her chest. She could hear and feel it throbbing in her ears. This woman's tongue was doing the most delightful things to her neck and when she kissed her again Noelle groaned and wrapped her arms around Sasha tightly.

When Sasha ended the kiss she took Noelle's hand and led them down the hall to her bedroom. Once inside she walked them to the foot of the bed and faced Noelle.

"I want you, Noelle, and it has nothing to do with our jobs or families or where we live. I want to touch this beautiful woman who has captivated my thoughts, and I want you to touch me," she said softly, looking intensely into her eyes. "I don't want to push any of these emotions away. I want to live in them. I want to share them with you."

Noelle could see the want in Sasha's eyes and her words went straight to her heart. She looked down at the flannel shirt Sasha was wearing and unbuttoned it. Then she eased it off her shoulders and gently ran her fingers along Sasha's collarbones. She had a weakness for collarbones and hers were damn near perfect. Her lips followed where her fingers traced and then she gently ran her tongue along the same sensitive path.

"Mmm, Noelle," Sasha whispered, letting her head fall back.

Noelle smiled and then took a moment to appreciate the black lace bra. She hoped Sasha could see in her eyes how much she liked it. "We only get one first time and I want to savor every moment, every touch, every feeling we share."

Sasha nodded and found the bottom of Noelle's shirt and raised it over her head. Noelle watched Sasha's eyes light up when she saw the beautiful red bra that Noelle was wearing. "Did you wear that for me?"

Noelle nodded and smiled. "It's time to get these clothes off." She reached for Sasha's jeans and unbuttoned them and slid the zipper down. Then she slowly lowered them as she trailed her hands down the sides of Sasha's legs. She let her step out of them and before standing back up, she cupped Sasha's firm cheeks and kissed her stomach. Then she pressed the side of her face where her lips had just been and inhaled Sasha's warmth. She became aware that Sasha's fingers were now entwined in her hair.

Noelle stood and began to take her own pants off. Sasha stopped her. "Let me," she said, pulling her pants down and then running her fingers underneath the band of her matching lace panties. "These are beautiful, but they have to go," she said, gazing into her eyes.

Noelle tipped her head, giving her permission to take them off. In one motion Sasha had her underwear gone and then unhooked her bra. Noelle's small round breasts were freed and Sasha saw her hardened nipples.

"You are gorgeous," Sasha said softly, gazing into her eyes.

Noelle reached around and unhooked Sasha's bra and slowly slid the straps down, revealing the most beautiful breasts she'd ever seen. "Oh Sasha," she whispered. With both hands holding Sasha's face she kissed her gently, but then deepened the kiss, pulling her close. Their chests met and Noelle could feel the firm softness of Sasha's breasts against hers and moaned.

As soft and slow as they began, their kisses became more urgent and their hands roamed.

Sasha pulled away and led them around to the side of the bed. She pushed Noelle gently down and then eased on top of her. Their lips met and Noelle sank into the kiss. She could feel Sasha everywhere. Her body was pressed to hers, her leg rested between Noelle's legs, and her hand was once again in her hair.

"Mmm," Sasha moaned as she began to kiss Noelle's neck. She ran her tongue up until she found her ear and swirled her tongue around and inside.

"Oh God," Noelle moaned as her hands roamed up and down Sasha's back.

"I intend to taste every inch of you," Sasha said as she alternated kisses and licks down to Noelle's breast. She circled her nipple with her tongue and then sucked it into her mouth while her hand cupped the other one. Next she kissed her way over to the other breast and gave it the same attention. Several moments and groans later she looked up into Noelle's eyes with a smile.

Noelle gently ran her hand over Sasha's hair as they stared. Something connected inside them because Sasha raised up and brought their lips together in a soul affirming kiss. Her hand stroked up and down Noelle's side and then lower to her thigh and under her leg. When she reached the inside of Noelle's thigh she bent her leg at the knee and let it fall open. She wanted Sasha inside her!

Sasha's fingers found Noelle's wetness and they both moaned. She stroked her finger through Noelle's folds and up and around her clit.

"You are so wet," whispered Sasha.

"You do that to me," moaned Noelle. "Please, Sasha, I need you inside me."

"That's where I want to be," Sasha said breathlessly.

She circled Noelle's opening and pushed inside. "Oh God," Noelle moaned. "Yes!" She could feel Sasha's smile against her neck and then she began a rhythm with those magical fingers that filled Noelle with such pleasure.

Sasha's lips found hers again and this kiss was hot and firm and their tongues became tangled as their rhythm sped up. Noelle's arms tightened around Sasha as she came closer to falling into the bliss of the orgasm that Sasha was building inside her.

"So good," Noelle murmured as her hips moved in perfect rhythm.

Sasha sped up her hand again and said gently, "Let go. It's okay to let go."

Noelle felt like she was speaking to her soul and with one more kiss Sasha's fingers stilled inside her and curled just enough to make Noelle see stars behind her closed eyes as she moaned into her lover's mouth.

She tore her mouth away and held Sasha tight as wave after wave of pleasure swept through her. When she couldn't hold on any longer she relaxed her arms and groaned. "Sasha," she said, the word coming out as a whisper.

"Take a breath, honey, because I'm not nearly through with you," Sasha said as she began to kiss her way down between Noelle's legs.

"Oh!" Noelle said when Sasha began to lap up her wetness.

"I told you I was going to taste every inch of you," Sasha said, looking briefly into her eyes.

"Mmm," she moaned. "That feels heavenly." She thought she was spent, but it didn't take Sasha but a few licks with that magical tongue to have Noelle ready to fall again, this time even harder. It was quick and intense, but oh so good.

She tugged on Sasha's head and had her rest it on her chest as her breathing began to calm.

"That was amazing, incredible, pick an adjective," Noelle said, stroking her hand over Sasha's head.

Sasha chuckled against Noelle's chest. "*You* are amazing, incredible, pick an adjective. And we're just getting started."

"Oh God. Merry fucking Christmas to me," Noelle said then chuckled.

12

"You don't get to have all the fun," Noelle said as she rolled on top of Sasha.

Sasha chuckled. "That wasn't fun for you?"

"Oh my God, Sasha. I hope I can show you just how good that was."

She smiled. "You already did. Your body's response told me everything."

"Not quite all," Noelle said with a sexy smile. "I know you liked this," she said, beginning to kiss and lick across Sasha's collarbones again.

Sasha could feel goosebumps rise on her chest. "I think your tongue is what I like," she said as her breathing began to pick up. She felt Noelle's smile on her skin.

"We'll see about that," she mumbled as she circled Sasha's nipple with her tongue. Then she sucked it into her mouth and bit down gently.

Sasha felt a gush of wetness to her core when Noelle's teeth tugged on her nipple. "Ahh," she moaned.

Noelle continued to lavish both of Sasha's breasts with

kisses and affection, then she came up and looked into Sasha's eyes.

"Watch," she whispered. When she saw Sasha's eyes on her finger she started just below Sasha's breast and ran it down so softly and gently to her hip bone. Then she trailed it across and below her stomach to her other hipbone.

Sasha gasped and bit down on her bottom lip.

Noelle's gentle touch circled back around and she did it again.

Sasha's chest was rising and falling rapidly as she tried to take a breath. She knew when Noelle met her eyes she could see the desire burning in them because she claimed her lips possessively and kissed her with purpose. The kiss was so intense Sasha didn't at first feel Noelle flatten her hand and run it down her thigh and back up until it rested on her center. But then she felt those fingers spread her lips and join the heat and wetness already pooled there.

She spread her legs wider because she wanted this woman like she'd never wanted anyone before. The fire Noelle built inside her was raging and she needed to be touched. Noelle's fingers caressed, explored, and pressed.

"Yes, Noelle. Yes," Sasha moaned, moving her head from side to side. "I want," she breathed. "I want all of you." The frenzy Noelle invoked in her had to be fulfilled.

Noelle began to kiss, bite, and lick down her body until Sasha thought she might scream. But when Noelle pushed two fingers inside her and sucked her clit into her mouth, Sasha felt all the euphoria she knew Noelle was leading her to.

"Ohhhh, yes!" she moaned.

Then Noelle used the magic they were creating to make Sasha's body sing. She flattened her arms on the bed but then reached for Noelle's hair. This was everything. Their rhythm was perfect. Noelle brought her closer and closer until she couldn't hang on any longer.

She pushed in and found Sasha's ultimate spot and at the same time she whispered, "I've got you." Then she kissed her as Sasha's scream flew down her throat and into her heart.

They held one another for several moments before Sasha finally relaxed into the bed letting out a huge exhale.

"Good God, Noelle," she said softly, running her hand up and down her back.

Noelle lifted her head and looked into Sasha's eyes.. From the moment they'd met, Sasha had felt like she could tell her anything. She trusted those eyes and this woman with no good reason to do so. This felt like so much more than just sex and getting to know one another. Should she speak the feelings into existence?

"Tell me," Noelle said softly.

Sasha cupped the side of her face and studied those green eyes a moment more as they sparkled and twinkled, telling her it was okay to be honest.

"That was magical," she said shyly.

Noelle smiled and gazed into Sasha's eyes. "Do I hear a hint of surprise? Because I felt it too."

Sasha visibly softened. *Thank goodness.* "Something has happened to me since you came to town," she said. "I don't know if it's that enchanted Christmas tree you sold me or this mystery surrounding decorated Christmas trees appearing around town or those wonderfully gay rainbow ornaments on all the trees."

"Is it a bad thing?" Noelle asked playfully.

"No! It's just that it's surprising and out of the ordinary and so unexpected."

"Oh." Noelle grinned. "You're in a small town where

things are slow and predictable—or at least they're supposed to be." She propped her head on her elbow and entwined their fingers with her other hand.

"Well yeah. I never imagined..."

Noelle squeezed her hand. "Neither did I."

"What are we going to do about it?" Sasha whispered.

"We're going to spend Christmas together," said Noelle.

"What?"

"All of the things you mentioned are magical and that's hard for your analytical, disciplined mind to understand. You said something has happened to you; well, Christmas magic is real in Santa Junction."

"You believe in Christmas magic?" Sasha said skeptically.

"It's inside me. I was born in Santa Junction!"

Sasha pushed Noelle down beside her. They faced one another and she looked into her eyes. "Then you have to believe that there's still Christmas magic here for you."

Noelle looked at her with confusion.

"I know you don't feel happy when you come home now because of your mom. If you brought that magic to me then I know it's still here for you." Sasha could see Noelle's eyes soften and she couldn't keep from kissing her. This woman had somehow snuck into her heart and now she cared. She wanted those gorgeous green eyes to sparkle just for her.

Before she realized what was happening she was once again on top of Noelle, kissing her heatedly. She couldn't stop her heart now even if she wanted to. How did this happen? *Who cares!* Right now all she could think about was kissing Noelle Winters in all the best places.

Sometime later Sasha chuckled as Noelle's head rested on her stomach.

"What's funny?"

"Did you think this was how you'd spend your Sunday?"

Noelle giggled. "I wasn't sure."

"What?" Sasha looked down at her. "You didn't think we'd end up in bed all afternoon and into the evening?"

"Not exactly. What I did know was that I wanted more kisses and I was pretty sure where that would lead us."

"I like where it leads us," said Sasha, gently combing her fingers through Noelle's thick auburn locks. "But I have worked up quite a hunger. How about you?"

Noelle raised up and grinned. "Oh yeah, the hunger you awakened in me is immense."

Sasha chuckled, knowing she wasn't talking about food.

"But I could eat a bowl of that delicious soup you made yesterday."

"With your bread," added Sasha.

They quickly dressed and went to the kitchen.

"I'm going to be sore in the best places tomorrow," Sasha said, taking down two bowls. She got the soup from the refrigerator while Noelle unwrapped the bread.

"Well if you hadn't made me so hungry," teased Noelle.

"Me? You had me practically begging." Sasha laughed. Then she turned Noelle around and pushed her against the counter. "And I never beg," she added, kissing her thoroughly.

Noelle didn't let Sasha go when the kiss ended. "Would you like to cook dinner with me in my kitchen tomorrow night?"

"I thought you were going to take me to a restaurant of my choice."

Noelle quirked an eyebrow.

"Yeah, we can go to a restaurant anytime."

"That's what I thought."

They both laughed and went back to preparing the soup and bread.

13

The next morning Sasha sat down at her desk and smiled. Her thoughts had been on Noelle all morning. She couldn't get this woman out of her head and didn't want to. Glancing down at her calendar to see what she had scheduled for the day made the smile fall from her face.

"Dang School Board meeting," she muttered. She got her phone and texted Noelle.

You had me in such a haze of sexual bliss yesterday I didn't remember that I have to cover the School Board Meeting tonight for the paper. I could come by before the meeting?

She waited and immediately saw the three little dots appear telling her Noelle was typing.

Are you suggesting a quickie?

Sasha giggled and immediately began her response.

I don't see 'that' being something we ever do quickly. I like seeing you in your clothes as well as out of them. However...

She sent the message and giggled again. This was fun. She couldn't remember the last time she'd flirted via text messages. Her eyes didn't leave the screen as she anxiously awaited Noelle's reply.

"Good morning," Rita said, plopping down in the chair across from her desk. "Who is putting that smile on your face? Please tell me it's Noelle."

Sasha looked up at her good-intentioned nosy friend and decided she couldn't hide Noelle from Rita even if she tried. Before Sasha could say anything her phone pinged with Noelle's reply.

I'll be waiting whenever you get here. With or without clothes. You'll just have to 'come' and see.

Sasha laughed and began typing her response. "Just a moment, Rita."

Can't wait.

She put her phone down and exhaled. She looked across at Rita and narrowed her eyes. "Noelle is indeed responsible for this smile. We had a lovely weekend."

Rita's eyes widened. "Weekend?"

"We had dinner Saturday and then I had lunch with her family and she gave me a tour of her house yesterday," she explained.

"Isn't that the cutest little house," said Rita.

"It is."

Rita had such a pleased look on her face. "When are you seeing her again?"

If she only knew how much of Noelle I've seen, she thought, trying to keep the evil grin off her face. "This evening."

Rita nodded and gave her an appraising look, then began to smile. "I could cover the School Board Meeting. There is nothing of much interest on the agenda."

"You'd do that for me?"

Rita leaned forward and looked at Sasha sincerely. "I'll

do whatever I can to help you give Noelle a reason to come home."

Sasha furrowed her brow. "Why do you think I could get her to stay?"

Rita shook her head. "Sometimes love is blind."

"What?" Sasha said, shocked.

"You and Noelle are perfect for one another. You have seen the same horrors, want to improve people's lives, and you need each other."

"Need each other?"

"Yes," Rita said with a kind smile. "You both are searching for the same thing. And I think you probably already know you've found her."

Sasha couldn't deny that after Noelle had left last night, she'd thought about how she suddenly found Noelle Winters in her heart. Could you fall in love in one day? It had been a while since she'd had sex with anyone and she wanted to attribute her feelings to the amazing orgasms they'd shared, but she knew it was more than that. When she looked into Noelle's eyes she knew she felt it too.

"Why doesn't she want to come home? Is it all because of her mom? And why do you want her here so bad?"

Rita sat back and sighed. "Noelle was very close to her mom. I think it hurts her heart when she comes here because she sees her everywhere. If she would just stay around long enough, she could get past that and begin to see her mom in happy ways. It doesn't help that the job she has is in a way a memorial to her mom."

"What? I thought she'd had that job for twenty years."

"She has. When she took the job her mom was so proud. She was helping people just like Holly did. It started as a job when she first got out of college until she could decide what she wanted to do. You see, Holly was the school counselor for years and Noelle also got her master's degree in counseling. She planned to take a year and go back to school and get her PhD, but that never happened."

"Because she loved her job?"

"Yes, she loved helping others and of course it made her family proud. But she didn't get to come home much which wasn't so bad for her. Coming out was hard back then because our town was run by homophobic old men."

"She mentioned that to me," said Sasha, listening closely.

"After the years passed I think she stayed in the job because she didn't know what else to do. She was obviously very good at it and it was kind of following in Holly's footsteps of helping others."

"But then her mom died."

"Exactly. I think part of the reason she doesn't come home now is because maybe she thinks she should have all those years ago. I don't know for sure. All I know is that she should be here. She needs this town and this town needs her."

Sasha didn't say anything as she took in all that Rita said.

"Okay, this is going to sound weird, but Santa Junction has always been a magical little place. You can feel it especially this time of year. The magic is in the people," she said, staring at Sasha. "Certain people."

Sasha looked at her with raised eyebrows and waited.

"Holly was one of those people. Noelle is one of those people. It's almost as if when she gets here the town cheers up. Have you noticed a difference since she's been here?"

Sasha thought about this. "I can't answer that objectively because I've noticed a difference in me since she got here."

"In small places like this there are always some people

that are the backbone of the town. They can be born here or move in. Some have been here for generations, like Noelle's family, or they've come here and want to make a difference, like you."

"Oh, I don't know about that," Sasha said.

"Some folks can't handle the responsibility and move on or they embrace it and love it, like Nick. Noelle would too, if she'd stay."

"Even though the town hurt her when she was young?"

"Her family and their friends stood by her and saw how the town needed to progress and they did. Noelle would do the same..."

"If she would stay," Sasha said, finishing Rita's sentence. "I realize this is a small town, but why are you putting so much of this on Noelle? That seems like a burden."

"It's not for the town; it's for her," said Rita. "She needs to come home for herself."

"I'm not sure why you're telling me all this," said Sasha.

"You like her. I could see it the day I introduced you. Aren't you a little bit afraid to get involved with her if she's going to leave after Christmas?"

The thought had crossed Sasha's mind and that's why she was so surprised that she already had feelings for her. But Noelle said they would spend Christmas together, that it would be magical.

When Sasha didn't answer Rita continued. "I think Santa Junction has chosen to sprinkle a little bit of magic on you. I know you've traveled a lot and could have settled down anywhere and yet here you are. Isn't it curious that Noelle made it home shortly after you arrived? And isn't it interesting that you both have been to so many of the same places at *almost* the same time? Seems a bit magical that you both end up here at the *same* time, wouldn't you say?"

Sasha smiled. Rita had given her plenty to think about. "I appreciate the offer to cover the meeting, but I have to give an update on the mentor program. "

Rita nodded and gave her a smile before getting up and going to her desk.

At first the Christmas Tree Mystery and all the magical talk was amusing. And then she bought her own tree and teased about it being magical, but was it? Is that what she was feeling whenever she was around Noelle? Sasha shook her head to clear the thoughts. All of a sudden she felt like she was in a fucking Hallmark Christmas movie.

* * *

Noelle smiled when she read the text from Sasha.

"I'm going to guess that's from Sasha," said Lisa as she filled Noelle's coffee mug.

Noelle chuckled and quickly responded to her text. "We're supposed to make dinner at my place tonight, but she forgot about the School Board meeting. I think she's going to stop by before."

"Uh huh. You must have had a good time decorating yesterday."

"Oh shit, I'm glad you said that. She saw all those decorations for the Christmas trees at my place yesterday. She offered to help me with mine. I've got to get rid of some of those; there's way too many of the same thing. By the way, you covered it quite well when she asked you to help with the investigation."

"Would it be so bad if she found out it was you?" asked Lisa.

"No. I just don't want the town to know," said Noelle. She looked at her sister-in-law who was also one of her closest friends. "I thought this would be the last year for the trees. I wanted to pass it on to Belle and let her keep up the tradition," she added tentatively.

"And what are you going to do? Watch her while you're home?" Lisa scoffed.

"No. I wasn't coming home," she said softly.

"What?"

"I thought you could all visit me during the year and I wouldn't come home for Christmas."

"That's the dumbest thing I've ever heard."

Noelle's brows shot up her forehead.

"I know you miss Holly, Noelle. We all do. And Christmas isn't the same without her, but did you ever think that *we* want you here? It wouldn't be the same without you either. Why would you do that to us? You'd better rethink whatever it is going through that head of yours."

Noelle's phone pinged again with Sasha's text. She smiled as she replied.

"I can see in your eyes that you care about Sasha. It doesn't matter that you've only known each other a short time. Why in the world would you do that to her?"

"I have been shocked by Sasha. I can't believe what's happening between us. She is just as surprised as I am."

"Then don't fuck up this chance! If anyone is ever going to get you, Noelle, it's her. She's shared the experiences you have. She understands."

"If I've learned anything from going into devastated areas to help people rebuild their lives it's what's precious. It isn't things and possessions, it's people and how they make you feel and you make them feel. It's sharing your heart, it's love. That's what's precious and what they said over and over." Noelle's shoulders dropped.

"You need to stop hiding from your mom's memory and

live in it instead. I happen to know that the high school counselor is not coming back after Christmas. That would be such a nice way to honor your mom's legacy and begin your own. This town is in you and it's calling for you. Why do you think Sasha Solomon showed up here out of the blue? It's Santa Junction magic with a little of your mom's magic thrown in."

"What?"

"I know you feel it. You both mentioned the near misses you had all these years and now when you are both ready for something new you end up in the same town. And not just any town."

Noelle knew there was something magical between her and Sasha. She had felt it the day they met, but thought it was just the excitement of being home. Yesterday Sasha reached deep inside her and held her soul. Noelle told her they would spend Christmas together and it would be magical.

"I'd better get my house ready for a visit later," she said, finishing her coffee.

"What tree are you and Belle decorating tonight?"

"I thought we'd do one at the high school for mom," she said, putting her mug in the sink.

"They have cameras. Wear your masks," Lisa said.

"Thanks, we will."

"Will you think about what I said?" asked Lisa.

"No need to, Lisa. I'm going to let the magic happen."

Lisa smiled at her and gave her a hug.

"What was that for?"

"I can't hug my sister-in-law when she's being smart for a change?"

Noelle laughed. "I love you, too."

14

Noelle squeezed lime over the chicken as her phone pinged with a text message.

I'm here! You'd better get those clothes off.

She laughed and went outside to see Sasha walking with purpose across the yard.

She stopped and held up her arms. "What's this?"

Noelle laughed and pulled her close for a kiss. She felt Sasha's arms tighten around her shoulders as she sank deeper into it.

"That's what I've been missing today," she said with a sultry smile on her face. "But you have clothes on," she added, changing her tone.

"I had a better idea." Noelle led her into the house.

"It smells heavenly in here," Sasha said, eyeing the food on the counter.

"I knew you wouldn't have time to eat before the meeting, so I made tacos."

"Oh, so food is more important than sex," Sasha teased, taking a chip from the basket.

Noelle chuckled. "No. Sit and I'll explain." She scooted a

stool towards Sasha. She released a latch and pulled out an extension on the cabinet that turned into a small table.

"Whoa, isn't that ingenious," Sasha said with delight in her voice.

Noelle laid out a makeshift taco bar between them. There were soft tortillas, shredded chicken, and toppings of lettuce, tomatoes, and cheese. She handed Sasha a plate. "Dig in."

"This is amazing," she said, building a taco. "When did you have time to cook during your travels?"

"You'd be surprised the things I learned," Noelle said, filling her plate.

"Are these homemade tortillas?"

"They are. I learned how to make them from a wonderful woman in Haiti." Noelle waited for Sasha to take a bite and was not disappointed by her reaction.

"Mmm, this chicken," she mumbled while she chewed.

"I know! It's delicious, isn't it? She taught me that, too," Noelle said with a pleased smile on her face.

After a few satisfying bites Sasha wiped her mouth and gave Noelle an appraising look. "You've been holding out on me, Noelle Winters. Can you imagine the fun we could have cooking together in my kitchen?" she asked, taking another bite.

Noelle grinned. "We had a lot of fun in your bedroom yesterday," she murmured.

Sasha laughed. "What's your better idea?"

"Well," Noelle said, wiping her mouth. "I have these decadent pralines for dessert."

She showed them to Sasha and when she reached for one Noelle pulled it away. "Not so fast."

Sasha looked at her with amusement. "Okay..."

"My mom used to get so many of these every Christmas. She used them as stocking stuffers and little gifts for her co-workers. I ordered a few this year to surprise Nick's family, but I happen to have my own stash," she said in a hushed voice.

Sasha's eyebrows crept up her forehead. "Oh, so you'd share one from your stash with me?" She sat back and eyed Noelle. "That must mean you like me," she said.

"You are figuring it out." Noelle nodded. "But you have to come back after the meeting to share dessert with me."

"Oh," said Sasha, grinning. "That seems like a win-win for me."

"How so?"

"I get to see you again *and* have dessert. One question?"

"Yes?" Noelle said, drawing the word out.

"Are you or the praline dessert?"

Noelle's green eyes twinkled. "What do you think?" She leaned over slowly and kissed her.

"Mmm," Sasha purred. "Now it's getting interesting."

"So you'll come back?" Noelle said with her lips almost against Sasha's.

"What do you think?" Sasha pressed her lips to Noelle's. She leaned back and made another taco. "These are so good," she mumbled.

"I'm glad you like them."

Sasha took another bite and stared at Noelle as she chewed. She wiped her mouth and asked, "What are you going to do while I'm at the meeting?"

"Belle is coming over. We get together once a week to watch a couple of TV shows we like."

Sasha nodded.

"She'll be gone by the time you get here."

"Are you sure I'm not messing up your plans?"

"You are my plans, remember? I did invite you over for dinner."

"I'm really sorry about the meeting. I totally forgot, which is all your fault," Sasha said, giving her a playfully menacing look.

Noelle laughed. "I take full responsibility, but I had help."

Sasha joined her laughter. She leaned toward Noelle. "I loved yesterday."

Noelle replied, "I did too." She looked at Sasha's lips and had to have them on hers. She reached her hand across the small table, grabbing Sasha's neck and pulling their lips together. This wasn't a soft kiss like before. This was a kiss full of what was to come. Her tongue slipped between Sasha's lips, filling them both with a blast of pleasure. She could feel the electricity fly down to her toes and back up, landing right between her legs.

"Oh fuck," she moaned.

Sasha smiled. "Yeah," she said, out of breath.

"That's what will be waiting for you after that meeting," said Noelle.

Sasha stared and Noelle could see how her warm brown eyes had darkened. She imagined her green ones looked the same way.

"I'd better go," said Sasha. "Let me help you clean up real fast."

"No, I've got it," said Noelle, clearing the table and sliding it back into the cabinet.

"That is so cool," said Sasha.

"Hey," Noelle said, putting her arms around Sasha's neck. "I'm glad you came over and I can't wait for you to come back."

Sasha put her hands on Noelle's hips and around her

middle, tugging her closer. They were gazing dreamily into each other's eyes and Noelle felt a sense of love. Instead of scaring her it was comforting and hopeful. She wondered if Sasha felt it too, but then she could see it in her eyes. It felt a little magical, but mostly it felt honest and true.

Then their lips met and Noelle could taste it. This kiss was warm and trusting and then it got hot. Tongues began to touch then battle. Their arms tightened and breaths came in gasps. Lips nibbled and nipped. Moans turned into groans and they tore their lips away from each other, but they didn't let go.

They were nose to nose, panting and staring. *This must be what it's like when hearts speak*, thought Noelle. Their breathing started to calm, but still they held tight.

Finally able to speak, Sasha said softly, "I'll be back as soon as I can."

Noelle nodded and began to smile.

They shared one more quick kiss and then walked out the door hand in hand to Sasha's car. Noelle opened the door for her, but before she got in Sasha pulled her close. "Thank you for dinner. I'll be back for dessert."

"You're welcome," Noelle said quietly. She released a loud exhale and stepped back so she could get in the car.

Sasha backed out and Noelle gave her a little wave. "What the fuck," Noelle said breathlessly. Then she smiled and walked back to her house humming.

"That looked pretty damn hot, Auntie," said Belle, walking out of her parent's back door.

"Shit, Belle."

"Sorry, I didn't mean to startle you. I can't imagine what you were thinking about," she said, grabbing her aunt around the neck.

Noelle laughed.

"So what's this big change all about tonight?"

"We're taking your mom's car and we're decorating in thirty minutes," said Noelle as they walked into her house.

"It's kind of early isn't it? Where are we going?"

"Right outside your classroom window."

"What?"

"Yeah, I want to do a tree at the high school and there's one outside your window."

"Why so early?"

"Because I have plans later," said Noelle, getting a bag with decorations from her bedroom.

"Uh huh, what kind of plans?" teased Belle.

Noelle chuckled. "I think you know," she said, rummaging in the bag. "Hey, have you seen my other glove? I found one in the bag, but not the other."

"I put them in the bag that night at the park."

"Maybe it's in my car. Oh well, I've got another pair somewhere."

"What's the plan?"

"Hoodies and masks tonight because they have cameras. We'll park a block away and walk in."

"I have everything in my car. So, tell me about Sasha."

Noelle looked at her niece and could see she was genuinely interested, not teasing. "She's amazing. I knew who she was, but she's so much more. I feel so comfortable around her, like I've known her forever. It's hard to explain. It feels like we're supposed to be together. It feels right. That sounds like a romance novel doesn't it?"

Belle chuckled. "Who cares what it sounds like? If it makes you happy, that's what's important."

"It does make me happy. So much so that I might hang around awhile," said Noelle.

Belle's face lit up with surprise. "That would make me so happy," she said, hugging her aunt.

Noelle laughed. "We'll see. I think we've waited long enough. Let's go."

They got in Lisa's car and drove to Santa Junction High School.

"What are all these cars doing here?" said Belle.

"Shit! They must be having the School Board meeting here tonight," said Noelle.

They drove around the area and then around the west side of the school.

"I think everyone is inside," said Noelle. "This might still work."

Belle peered out the window. "I think you're right. I don't see a soul. Let's drive in front and see if anyone is in the foyer. They must be having the meeting in the auditorium."

Noelle turned to drive in front of the school. "Lean back from the window. I know they have cameras pointed at the street."

Belle did as she was told and looked at the front door as they drove by. "It looks clear. Everyone must be inside."

"I didn't see anything on this side either. Okay, I'm going to drive down a block and we'll walk back up. If we see anyone we'll turn and keep going."

"Got it."

Noelle parked the car and Belle got the bag from the backseat. They walked up the sidewalk and when they approached the school they pulled their hoodies up and put their masks on. The tree was also on the north side which was the front of the building, but it was down from the entrance.

"Let's stay near the building until we get even with the tree," Noelle said quietly.

Belle walked behind her and they paused when they reached the tree. "All clear."

"Let's do it. This one's for Momma," Noelle whispered.

They went to work and strung the lights quickly. Belle started hanging ornaments and gave Noelle the star.

"It's your turn," said Belle.

Noelle smiled behind her mask and bent the branch down to attach the star. She let the branch go slowly and the star stood tall. Then she hung the rainbow ornament right in front. Belle made sure there was no trash left on the ground and grabbed the bag. They were about to turn the lights on when they saw a car coming.

"Hurry to the building," said Noelle in a loud whisper.

They ran and flattened themselves against the building while the car drove by. Its lights illuminated the tree, but not them. If they'd stayed by the tree they would have been seen. Once it was out of sight they waited a few moments and Noelle ran back to the tree to turn the lights.

She didn't take time to admire this one. Instead she hurried back to the building and she and Belle walked quickly alongside it then down the street in the opposite direction of the car.

When they had walked a block further they began to relax. They turned down another street and started back towards the car.

"Whew, that was a little close," said Belle.

"Yeah it was."

"But I have to say, it was fucking exciting!" she said, punching her aunt in the arm.

"We're not to the car yet. I'll feel better when we're driving away."

Five minutes later they closed the doors, Noelle started the car, and they drove off.

"Now do you feel better?"

"Yes, I can breathe," said Noelle.

"Let's drive by and see the lights. Go the opposite direction from where we came in."

Noelle turned in front of the school and drove from east to west this time. The lights were shining bright.

Belle laughed with glee. "Look! Everyone will be able to see it when they leave the meeting. Mimi would love that."

"Yeah she would. Spreading Christmas cheer, my dear niece," Noelle said, holding out her hand. Belle slapped it and Noelle drove them home.

She couldn't wait for Sasha to get there.

15

Sasha hurried to Noelle's house after the meeting. She couldn't wait to tell her about the decorated Christmas tree that was discovered in the front of the high school when the meeting adjourned. But more than that she couldn't wait for what that earlier kiss had promised. This may all be moving at lightning speed, but there was something about Noelle Winters that felt familiar. Then it hit her. Noelle felt like home. She had never felt that with anyone before. There certainly hadn't been a place she could ever call home and she had always hoped that someday she would feel it in somebody.

She shook her head and slowed those thoughts down. "You're getting way ahead of yourself," she said aloud. Maybe it was all this talk of Christmas magic. It didn't matter right then because she pulled into Noelle's driveway and quickly texted her.

I'm here for my dessert!

She giggled when she read Noelle's response and hurried to her door.

Come on in, I'm in the bedroom.

She opened the door and called out, "I'm here."

"Are you taking your clothes off?" she heard Noelle say from the bedroom.

She peeked inside the room and found Noelle sitting on the bed. The mistletoe that Sasha had brought her yesterday was hanging above the bed and Noelle held a praline.

"Your pick," said Noelle with the sexiest smile Sasha had ever seen. She was surprised her clothes didn't fall right off her body.

Sasha gave her a sexy smile back as she placed her hand on her hip and jutted it out. "You have clothes on."

"I said your pick?"

Sasha chuckled as she threw her coat in the corner and kicked her shoes off. "I choose you!" They then raced to get their clothes off and, giggling, Sasha jumped on top of Noelle. "Wait, I have to tell you something first."

"I'm all yours."

"Hmm, I like the sound of that," Sasha said in a sultry voice. "Ugh, you are so distracting."

Noelle looked at her and grinned.

"You'll never guess what happened at the School Board meeting."

"Let's see," she said, looking up. "You're right. I have no idea."

"When we came out of the meeting one of the trees in the front of the school had been decorated for Christmas, complete with twinkling lights and—wait for it," she paused, her face amused.

Noelle looked at her wide-eyed with feigned anticipation.

"A rainbow ornament right in the front."

"How about that?"

"Our secret elf is getting bold."

"My mom was a counselor at the high school for years. She would've loved that."

Sasha smiled down at her. "Everyone was gathered around it smiling and talking and laughing."

"Would you say this Christmas elf is spreading cheer?"

"Definitely."

"Everyone needs a little extra Christmas cheer."

"I would love to share a little cheer with you," Sasha said, wiggling her eyebrows.

Noelle's face turned serious. "Would you stay with me tonight?"

"You won't care that I snore?"

Noelle smiled. "I'm sure it will be the cutest little snore I've ever heard."

"I can't think of anything nicer than waking up with you in the morning," Sasha said earnestly.

"Oh, I can think of a few nicer things. Like this," Noelle said, pulling her down for a sensual slow kiss.

"You know that kiss earlier had me thinking of all kinds of reasons to leave that meeting early."

"You're here now," Noelle said, gently caressing the side of Sasha's face.

"When you look at me like that..." she mumbled and pressed her lips to Noelle's.

There was no more talking. Touches, moans, heated breaths and kisses filled the room. Sasha began to claim Noelle's body as her own. She kissed her mouth with heat and passion and then she nibbled down her neck. She raised up and flung her dark hair back, grabbing Noelle's hands and pinning them to the bed on either side of her head.

She looked into Noelle's eyes with such intensity and whispered, "I know I keep telling you this, Noelle, you are beautiful. There is something inside you calling to me."

Noelle stared back and then simply said, "Take me."

Sasha did just that. She began a barrage of kisses that started with Noelle's lips that she couldn't get enough of and then landed on her chest. She kissed and licked and nipped her way to Noelle's breasts. She felt like she was feasting on the most delectable treasures in the world.

Noelle's moans of pleasure only encouraged her as she kissed lower and lower. She ran her tongue just above Noelle's curly hairs across her sensitive lower abs.

"Oh, Sash," she moaned.

Sasha had to smile at the shortened use of her name. But then she went back only to end up at her ultimate prize. She slowly licked up and down and around Noelle's wet, heated sex.

"Oh my God," she groaned, her fingers weaving through Sasha's hair.

"Mmm, you like that? So do I, my angel," murmured Sasha as she quickly looked up at Noelle. Her red hair was fanned out over the pillow and those green eyes were begging her for more. Sasha felt the wetness pooling between her own legs. This woman filled her with more want and desire than she knew she could feel.

She slid her tongue around and around Noelle's sensitive bud and gave her what she wanted by pushing one then two fingers inside her.

Noelle's satisfied moan was followed by, "Oh Sash, that is so good! You are so good."

Sasha began a slow rhythm as Noelle's hips joined in. She licked and then sucked Noelle's clit into her mouth, causing more groans of pleasure from Noelle.

"Please don't stop," she pleaded.

There was no way Sasha was stopping. This was heaven for her too. Together they were riding this wave of sensual bliss to a sharp precipice of sensations and emotions. The fireworks exploding in their bodies and hearts were creating love whether or not they were ready for it.

Sasha laid her head on Noelle's stomach while their breathing calmed. She could feel Noelle's fingers still gently moving through her hair. This woman lit something inside her and she didn't want it to ever go out.

"Don't be afraid, don't be afraid, don't be afraid," Noelle whispered over and over.

Sasha eased up to lie next to Noelle. She bent her elbow and rested her head in her hand and gently kissed Noelle's cheek. "Are you telling me or yourself?"

Noelle smiled and said, "Both. When you touch me, kiss me, look at me, it does something inside me I can't explain. It is something I haven't ever felt and although it's kind of scary it's also exciting." She looked into Sasha's eyes, clearly trying to find the words. "When you're not with me I'm wondering what we're going to do next and then when you are with me it's like opening what you wanted for Christmas. It's the most wonderful gift."

Sasha let Noelle's words sink in. That had to be the nicest thing anyone had ever said to her. Imagine being the thing someone wanted most for Christmas.

"Hey," Noelle said. "You called me your angel."

Sasha smiled. "I did. You are like the angel that lights the top of a Christmas tree. Your beautiful red hair gleaming at me, lighting my way. You're my angel."

Noelle sighed pleasantly.

"But I want my other dessert," said Sasha with a grin.

Noelle leaned in to kiss Sasha but she put her finger over her lips. "Not so fast."

Noelle looked at her, confused. "I thought..."

"I want that," Sasha said, chuckling. "But I also want that praline."

Noelle laughed and reached across her to the night stand and grabbed the praline. She rolled onto her back and began to unwrap the treat. She broke off a piece and held it to Sasha's mouth.

Sasha opened her mouth and took the bite, nibbling Noelle's finger in the process. Her eyes lit up when she tasted the praline. "This is delicious," she moaned.

Noelle grinned. "Told you." She broke off a piece for herself.

"You know I'm kind of envious of you," Sasha said, taking another bite of the praline.

"Why?" asked Noelle.

"You have a place you belong. Growing up all over the world means you don't have a place to go home to for things like Christmas. We had Christmas wherever my parents were living. This year they are at my sister's place in DC. I tried to tell myself that it was the people that mattered, not the place. My parents always said they didn't need a place because they belonged to each other. I haven't found my person, so I came looking for a place."

"And that's why you're here?"

"There's a comfort in the familiar and belonging. Don't you feel that when you come home or even when you're away and think about home? You belong here, Noelle. I can't imagine how wonderful that must feel."

"It does, but Santa Junction hasn't always been kind to me, Sasha. When I was young and came out in high school there were some parents that didn't want their daughters to be friends with me. There were people on the city council that tried to make it an ordinance that same sex couples couldn't get married in the city limits."

"Damn!"

"Yeah. I can't tell you how wonderful it felt when I went to college and found other gay people. It was like taking a deep breath."

"How was it when you came home after that?"

"I had my family and then as those old mean men were voted off the city council, the town evolved. Rita can tell you all about it. She was always a safe space for me if my parents weren't around."

"So Santa Junction is the happy hometown again for you?"

"Not exactly. For me, the town feels like if I come home I'll never get away."

"That sounds ominous. What do you mean?"

"It wouldn't be a bad thing to live here, but I knew if I did that I'd have to resign myself to the fact that I'd be alone."

"Why?" asked Sasha, her brow furrowed and then realization hit her. "Oh! There aren't many gay people in town so you thought you'd never find someone here."

Noelle nodded. "That seems to be changing though."

"You keep telling me about the magic in this town. Don't you think it works on you?"

Noelle smiled. "I think you're the magic. Can I have *my* dessert now?"

Sasha gave her a sexy smile. "These kisses might be too sweet?"

Noelle rolled over on top of her and pressed her lips to

Sasha's for a hungry kiss. "Don't be afraid of the magic, Sash. All my fears about Santa Junction are somehow gone."

Sasha held Noelle's face in her hands and looked deeply into her eyes. "I want your magic," she whispered. Then she pulled her down for a heated kiss. The time for talk was over. She wanted to feel Noelle everywhere.

16

The next morning Sasha kissed Noelle goodbye and went home to get ready for work. Noelle had insisted she make her a quick cup of coffee and sent her on her way with a blueberry muffin. But not before a little early morning delight.

Sasha had woken that morning with Noelle's arms around her. She sighed, remembering how delicious it felt when Noelle's hands began to roam and her lips kissed her neck. She rolled over and it was definitely a good morning.

When she got to work she called Lisa and asked if she could get the video footage from the high school security cameras. She wanted to look at the night before and see if the tree decorator had been captured in the video.

Lisa secured the video for her and invited her to meet at her house to look at it that afternoon. When Sasha pulled into the driveway she couldn't help but think of Noelle. She knew she was helping at the Christmas tree lot so she didn't go by her house first, but that didn't mean a smile wasn't on her face as she went to Lisa's back door.

"Hi," said Lisa. "Come in."

"Hi. Thanks for helping me on this," Sasha said graciously.

"No problem. Have a seat," she said, gesturing toward the kitchen table. "I was about to have a cup of coffee, would you join me?"

"I could use one." Sasha made herself comfortable at the table.

"Late night?" commented Lisa with a knowing smile as she made their coffee.

Sasha chuckled. "I guess you noticed my car in your driveway this morning."

Lisa grinned as she set a mug of coffee in front of Sasha. "I'd love to tease you about it, but I can't. I'm happy you and Noelle have found each other."

Sasha smiled. "It's so unexpected and a bit overwhelming."

"But good, right?" asked Lisa.

"Oh, it's so much better than good!" said Sasha, her face full of joy.

Lisa's laptop was sitting on the table. She sat next to Sasha and opened it. "I have never seen Noelle this happy."

"Really?"

"Really. She is very private with her love life and has never brought anyone home with her."

"My job was, in some ways, similar to hers and I can attest it can make a love life hard to maintain."

"In that respect I find it rather special that you've found one another here and at a time in your lives when a love life might be easier."

Sasha smiled. "You're not going to tell me it's Santa Junction magic, are you?"

Lisa laughed. "You don't believe in magic? Especially Christmas magic?"

"I didn't say that," said Sasha, joining her laughter. "But you're a detective that follows logic and clues so I wondered."

"Believe me, sometimes it takes luck and magic to solve cases."

Lisa found the file she was looking for on her computer and opened it. "This is the video from the camera in the front portico. It has the best view. This is around six o'clock."

Sasha looked on as the video showed people coming in the school for the meeting.

"Let me speed it up and you'll see what I discovered before you got here." Lisa ran the video forward and then returned it to regular speed. "This was about thirty minutes after the meeting started."

Sasha watched as a couple of cars drove in front of the school. There was nothing for several minutes and then two dark figures could be seen walking from the side of the building toward the tree.

"They came in from the east and walked next to the building so they wouldn't be seen from the street or by the other cameras," said Lisa as they watched two figures decorate the tree. They worked quickly and in sync.

"You can see that they run back to the building when the car comes. Then one goes back and turns the lights on while the other makes sure nothing is left behind," Lisa explained.

Sasha watched and couldn't shake the feeling that the figures looked familiar. She watched them hurry back to the building when a car drove down the street.

"Are they wearing hoodies?" she asked.

"Yes," Lisa replied.

"Could you run it again?" she asked.

"Sure." Lisa hit rewind and took the video back to where the two figures appeared on the screen.

Sasha watched and said, "It's obvious they are both women, which doesn't surprise me."

"Why is that?"

"I don't know. This feels like an emotional gesture." Sasha continued to watch and the way the taller woman moved seemed so familiar. When she pulled the branch down to put the star on the tree she watched how gently she let the branch go. "Have you tried to zoom in on their faces?"

"Yeah, it's too grainy."

"Could you play it one more time?"

Lisa backed the video up and let it play again. "Is there something you see?"

"No. This one," she said, pointing to the taller one. "She seems so familiar." As she watched, Noelle's voice ran through her mind: "Mom would have loved that. Maybe the person doesn't want to be thanked." Then she remembered being overcome with passion last night and burying her face in Noelle's thick hair. There was a fresh outdoor scent, but she'd forgotten to say anything.

Memories kept rolling through her head just like the video rolled across the screen. She watched as the other woman made sure there was nothing on the ground and remembered when she went to get a sprig of mistletoe to take to Noelle's, she'd found a glove next to the tree. She didn't think anything about it until she realized she'd seen the mate of that glove on Noelle's floor and picked it up.

Then the memory of buying ornaments for her tree came next. She saw Noelle buy two of the rainbow ornaments and remembered Mr. Hinson asked if she'd already purchased them. But then she gasped when it all made sense as she remembered meeting Belle and she said that her aunt had a way with Christmas trees. She remembered the look on Noelle's face as if her niece had said something she shouldn't have.

"Oh my God!" she exclaimed, looking over at Lisa.

The look on Lisa's face told her she was right.

"I know that's Noelle," she said, pointing to the taller woman. "And that's probably Belle."

"What makes you think that?" Lisa asked innocently.

Sasha lowered her chin and looked at Lisa with wide eyes. "I've come to know that body quite well," she deadpanned.

Lisa swallowed and stared at her. "Don't be mad."

"Mad? I'm not mad. I want to understand," Sasha said.

"Noelle's mom used to be the school counselor," she began.

"I know," Sasha interrupted. "She used to help families anonymously at Christmas." As she spoke the words she began to nod. "That's why she doesn't want anyone to know it's her. Is she doing this for her mom?"

"Yes. She wanted to honor her mom in some way. When she did the first one the whole town started talking. It spread Christmas cheer. The local paper and radio station ran contests on where the next tree would turn up."

Sasha smiled. "I imagine that made Noelle feel better."

"It did for the first couple of years, but not enough. She told me she wanted to turn it over to Belle and not come home at Christmas anymore."

Sasha furrowed her brow and her stomach dropped.

"But then you came along."

"And?" Sasha asked, her voice shaky.

"I think you've taken some of that sadness away."

"She told me that the reason she hasn't moved back here is because she didn't want to end up alone and she was afraid that would happen."

"She's not alone now, is she?"

Sasha smiled. "I want to know everything about her, Lisa. I've always heard about these connections people say they feel. I thought it was a bunch of bullshit until I met Noelle. I can't stop thinking about her." She sighed. "My family moved around a lot so I don't have a place like Santa Junction, a place that really feels like home. I always thought I would have someone, not just some place."

"Noelle is that someone, isn't she?"

"I feel like I've known her forever, but I want to know more. Does that make sense? I haven't told her, but I've fallen in love with her. I don't know what to do. She's through with her job. I can see it in her eyes when she talks about it. But how do I get her to stay here when she sees the ghost of her mother on every corner?" Sasha took a deep breath. "Rita thinks if she'll stay awhile she'll get past those sad memories and the happy ones will replace them."

Lisa nodded. "She's right. Deep down Noelle loves this town and it loves her."

"I want her to stay," said Sasha. "She likes to talk about the magic of Santa Junction. Rita thinks Holly and Noelle are magical too. I don't know how to explain why this is the town I ended up in or how I met Noelle and fell in love with her faster than the speed of light!"

Lisa chuckled. "I'd say faster than the speed of twinkling Christmas lights."

Sasha shook her head. "Surely you know how unreal this seems to an investigative journalist."

"I do, but I've been here over half my life and I've seen how magical this place can be. You're right in the middle of it! I think Santa Junction wants you both to stay."

Sasha looked at the video and tried to figure out what to

do next. Then she had an idea. "Do you know when they plan to decorate the next tree?"

"Let's see, she does five trees every Christmas. Last night was the third, wasn't it?"

Sasha nodded. "Yeah, there was the one on the town square, then the park and last night at the school. She did that one last night for her mom."

"Yes and for Belle. It's right outside Belle's classroom window."

Sasha chuckled. "How sweet is that!"

"I think they're doing the next one tomorrow night."

"Do you know where?"

"I don't see her as much as I used to for some reason," Lisa said, lightening the situation. "So I don't know for sure. I can find out."

Sasha nodded.

"What are you thinking?"

"Does she usually pick Belle up?"

"Yes, or they meet here."

"I want Belle to meet her there. Only Belle isn't going to show up. I am," said Sasha.

A smile grew on Lisa's face. "You want to take over for Belle?"

"I do."

Sasha hoped this worked, but if it didn't she fully intended to tell Noelle Winters she was in love with her and would go anywhere she wanted to go.

17

Noelle had just loaded a twelve foot Christmas tree in the back of a pickup when she turned and saw Lisa waiting for her.

"That was a big one," said Lisa. "I hope they have tall ceilings."

"They have a vaulted ceiling with the perfect spot for it according to Mrs. Phillips," Noelle said in a snooty accent.

Lisa laughed.

Noelle's tone turned serious when she said, "Could you tell on the video it was Belle and me?"

"Of course I could tell," said Lisa.

"You know what I mean," said Noelle in a stern whisper. "Does Sasha know?"

"She knows it's two women, but she already decided that before she saw the video."

"Really?"

"Yes. She thinks there is emotion attached to the reason the people are decorating the trees. You and Belle need to be careful. I think you need to split up."

“What do you mean, split up?” asked Noelle, her gaze narrowing.

“Where is the next tree?” Lisa asked quietly, looking over her shoulder to see if anyone was near them.

“I thought we’d do the one at the clinic. That’s a busy place this time of year and if anyplace needs cheer it’s the doctor’s office.”

Lisa nodded. “I think you need to meet there. You come in from one direction and have Belle meet you at the side of the building, near the corner. That spot is hard for cameras to reach.”

“Hmm.” Noelle considered Lisa’s words. “You’ve thought about this, Detective Winters.”

Lisa smiled. “I don’t want you to get caught.”

“Did Sasha mention the tip line on the website?”

“No. Why?”

“I just wondered if they’d received any more tips. She hasn’t mentioned it so I don’t think they have,” Noelle said, obviously in thought. Then she looked at Lisa and nodded. “Okay, that sounds like a good plan. I’ll tell Belle.”

“You won’t have to worry about your cars in that area. The only cameras are around the building.”

“Good to know. Thanks, Lisa. I appreciate this.”

“Have you thought about telling Sasha?” asked Lisa.

“Yeah, but there’s something more important I want to talk to her about first,” Noelle said, smiling.

Lisa studied her sister-in-law. “Something more important than Christmas trees?”

Noelle couldn’t contain the smile that grew on her face. Lisa was a detective; Noelle was pretty sure she’d figure it out.

“I think you two could have a happy life together, with or without Christmas trees,” she said.

"It's happened so fast," said Noelle.

"Not really. It's the magic of Santa Junction. You just both had to get here first." She smiled and walked back to her car.

Noelle watched her and sighed. She remembered talking about the magic of this place with Sasha. Rita used to tell her that her mom had Christmas magic inside her. It made her wonder if her mom had sent Sasha to her right when she needed her the most.

When Sasha got home from Lisa's she decided to take homemade hot chocolate to Noelle and surprise her while she sold trees. They had texted during the day and she knew the tree sales had been lively. It was colder tonight and she thought hot chocolate would be a nice way to warm her up until she could do it more privately.

She smiled while she stirred the rich liquid on the stove. Her thoughts took her back to when she'd admitted she was in love with Noelle. Lisa hadn't seemed to be surprised and was happy about it. She laughed out loud thinking about how Rita would react.

"I'm in love with Noelle Winters," she said, her voice bouncing around her kitchen. The words were easy to say and brought such fullness to her heart. She'd been in love before, but this felt different. There was no fear; she was sure that Noelle was in love with her too. The only problem was what Noelle wanted to do. Sasha was determined not to let Santa Junction be an issue. If she wanted to stay here they would. If not, Sasha wasn't going to lose her because of a town, magic or not.

She drove into the parking lot of the hardware store and

pulled around to the side where the temporary Christmas tree lot was set up. A smile immediately spread across her face when she saw Noelle helping a young couple choose a tree. Sasha could see the joy on her face as she explained the differences in the trees. She waited and watched her for a few more moments.

Should she question how fast and how hard they'd fallen for each other? She'd thought about this all day, but couldn't find one reason to slow down or not trust her heart. Who said you had to know someone for a specified amount of time before you could trust your feelings?

She would find out tomorrow how much Noelle trusted her when she showed up instead of Belle. There were times when she thought Noelle might explain more about her mom, but she'd always held back. Would she be angry or happy to see her? This might be the first test of their love.

She put that out of her mind as she got out of her car and walked to the back of the lot. When their eyes met, Noelle's face lit up like the Christmas trees she decorated.

"Hi gorgeous," Sasha said, leaning over and kissing her on the cheek.

"Hi yourself. What are you doing here?"

"I brought hot chocolate to warm you up." She handed Noelle a cup then poured from the thermos.

"Thank you," Noelle said. She tasted the drink and her face lit up again. "This is homemade."

"Only the best for you. The Christmas trees expect it." She winked.

Noelle looked at her, seeming confused.

"The trees you sell," Sasha clarified.

"Oh! Sorry." Noelle leaned in and said softly, "I was thinking of other ways you could warm me up."

Sasha chuckled. "Oh I know. This is just until you get home."

Noelle looked at her watch. "Only thirty more minutes."

"My place?" Sasha said with one eyebrow raised.

"You're not going to get tired of me?"

"How can you even ask that?" Sasha frowned.

Noelle quickly cupped Sasha's cheek and stared into her eyes. "I don't know how I got someone like you to want me. Sometimes it feels unreal."

"Kiss me, baby. I'm real and I'm right here."

Noelle pressed her lips to Sasha's and Sasha felt her heart speed up. She couldn't wait to get Noelle home. When Noelle pulled away Sasha said, "I'm all yours."

"I'll be at your place as soon as I can," Noelle said, her eyes glistening a very dark green. Sasha loved making her eyes dark like that.

"I'll be waiting." She kissed her again and gave her a smile that left no doubt what she had planned for her.

Noelle was about to knock on Sasha's front door when it opened. "Hey," she said, with her hand still in midair.

"Get in here," Sasha grinned, grabbing her hand and pulling her inside. "Your hand is cold as ice. Where are your gloves?"

Noelle remembered she hadn't found her other glove. She shrugged. "I left them at home." Her gaze traveled around the room and saw the Christmas tree lights twinkling and an inviting fire crackling in the fireplace. "What is all this?"

"I knew you'd be chilled from working outside most of the day and wanted to warm you up," Sasha said, leading her over to the couch. She poured them both a mug of cider and handed one to Noelle.

"Thank you," she said, taking the mug. She waited for Sasha to face her and then leaned in for a soft kiss. "This is nice."

Sasha leaned back and sighed. "It is."

Noelle rested back next to her and felt such a sense of comfort. It was that 'being exactly where you're supposed to be' feeling. She gently leaned her head over and rested it on Sasha's shoulder. "Did you think this was how it would be in Santa Junction?"

Sasha chuckled. "I never imagined I'd *be* in Santa Junction."

"How did you end up here?"

"I have a good friend that just happens to be one of the executives in the media corporation that owns the paper. He knew I was stepping away from the travel and being an every day correspondent and thought this might be a place for me to take a breath and consider my options, as he put it."

"How's that going so far?"

"Let's say my options are promising."

Noelle raised her head and looked into Sasha's eyes. "Remind me to thank your friend." Then she kissed Sasha tenderly. "Mmm, I'm full of magic since I sold Christmas trees all day." She cupped Sasha's face and gave her a sexy smile.

"Full of magic?" Sasha asked as she returned Noelle's smile. "Care to show me?"

Noelle set both their mugs on the table, stood and took Sasha's hand, pulling her to her feet. She led them down the hall to Sasha's bedroom. They each went to opposite sides of the bed and put the throw pillows on the floor. Their eyes sparkled as they pulled the bedspread back and then the blanket.

Sasha reached for the hem of her sweater and pulled it over her head. Her eyes never left Noelle's as she kicked her shoes off and slowly began to lower the zipper on her jeans. She stopped with her pants open and raised one eyebrow at Noelle.

Noelle could feel her heart pounding in her chest and her mouth went dry as Sasha slowly took her clothes off. She immediately understood the look Sasha gave her and unbuttoned her flannel shirt, dropping it to the floor. Her T-shirt was next and ended up somewhere behind her as she tossed it over her shoulder. She hurriedly pulled her boots off, then her jeans, and stood next to the bed waiting for Sasha to take her turn.

Sasha gave her a racy grin and shimmied out of her jeans. She reached behind her and waited for Noelle to mimic her posture. At the same time they unclasped their bras and let them fall.

"You are so beautiful, Sash," Noelle said quietly.

Sasha smiled and stared into Noelle's eyes. Her gaze fell to Noelle's naked chest and she took a deep breath. "Oh baby, so are you," she said, exhaling. Then she slowly lowered her undies and crawled onto the bed. She waited for Noelle in the middle on her knees.

Noelle slid her underwear down and joined Sasha. They faced each other, both on their knees. Noelle reached out and put her hand behind Sasha's neck, running her fingers through her hair. She fisted the dark, thick hair in her hand and pulled Sasha to her, their lips crashing into a heated kiss.

Their moans echoed around the room along with their ragged breaths. Noelle's other hand cupped Sasha's breast.

"That feels so good," groaned Sasha.

Noelle pinched Sasha's nipple and gasped when Sasha mirrored her movements. "Oh Sash," she moaned. Her lips found Sasha's and she kissed her with passion, but also with emotion. Noelle was falling for Sasha. She was in her heart and Noelle wanted her to stay there.

"I want you," she whispered into Sasha's ear, "and I want you to touch me."

Noelle ran her hand over Sasha's stomach and cupped her sex. Her middle finger slipped between her lips and met luxurious wet heat. She circled Sasha's swollen, throbbing bundle and they moaned in harmony.

"Fuck, Noelle," groaned Sasha. "Wait, let me," she said, running her hand down and into Noelle's sweet wetness.

They locked eyes and stroked each other, circling around and around and then they kissed. This kiss said what their voices weren't quite ready to speak.

Noelle slipped a finger inside Sasha and she groaned into her mouth.

"Baby," Sasha whispered as she pushed one finger then another inside Noelle.

They began a slow, sensual tempo while they stared into each other's eyes.

Noelle felt such pleasure, but she could see love in Sasha's eyes, too. At least she hoped that's what she saw. "This is so good, Sash," she said, closing her eyes.

"Look at me, baby," Sasha said, urging Noelle's eyes open. "I want to see those gorgeous green eyes when we–" she gasped, not finishing her sentence.

"When we come undone together," groaned Noelle.

Their pace quickened and Noelle could see Sasha's eyes darken and glisten. She didn't know how this amazing woman had come into her life—maybe it was magic. All she knew now was that she wanted Sasha to stay in her life.

Noelle kissed Sasha again and curled her fingers inside, brushing over her favorite spot.

Sasha tore her lips away and pulled Noelle closer with her other arm. Then she once again followed Noelle's lead and curled her fingers, sending Noelle into a massive orgasm.

Their eyes locked again and the electricity flowed from Noelle's body into Sasha's and spread all over and around them. Neither said a word, but the emotions running through them were visible and could be heard loud and clear. They held on until the last little shiver of pleasure left them weak.

Noelle began to smile and they fell over in the bed together. They rolled over onto their backs and stared at the ceiling for a moment.

Sasha began to laugh. "You *are* full of magic!" She rolled over and her hand fell on Noelle's stomach.

"That wasn't just me," said Noelle, facing Sasha.

"We're amazing," Sasha said softly.

"We are."

"Please stay with me tonight," Sasha said, cuddling up next to Noelle.

"I'm not going anywhere," she replied, putting her arm around Sasha and holding her close. She wasn't going anywhere tonight and had no plans to leave Santa Junction anytime soon.

18

"Did Noelle seem suspicious when you told her you'd meet her there?" asked Sasha.

"Nope," said Belle. "Mom did her best detective impression and easily convinced her it would be best to meet there."

"Impression?" Lisa said, sounding annoyed. "You seem to have forgotten that the money I earn as a detective paid for your college education."

"No I haven't, Mom!" said Belle. "I was just kidding."

Sasha chuckled at this exchange between mother and daughter and couldn't help imagining what it would be like to be in this family.

"See what I have to put up with?" said Lisa. "Aunt Noelle loves to take her favorite niece's side in everything. I need you to help me even things out."

Belle's eyes widened. "That would be so much fun!"

"Slow down, you two. Noelle may be very angry tonight when I show up instead of you."

"I don't think so, Sasha. I think in a way she'll be relieved," said Lisa.

Sasha sighed. "I hope she'll trust me enough to open up about her mom. I want to understand and help her if I can."

"You already have helped her," said Belle. "She hasn't been this happy even when Mimi was still here."

Sasha smiled. "I haven't been this happy since I don't know when, either."

Belle's phone pinged with a text message.

"It's time. She'll be waiting at the corner of the building," said Belle.

"You know where to go, right?" asked Lisa.

Sasha nodded.

"Okay, let's go," said Lisa.

When Lisa called Sasha earlier they decided that she would pick her up and take her to Belle's. They would await Noelle's text and then Lisa would drop Sasha a block from the clinic. That way she wouldn't have to worry about her car.

Sasha was nervous and kept taking slow deep breaths to calm her nerves. She knew Noelle would be surprised, but hoped she wouldn't be angry.

"It's going to be fine," Lisa said, glancing over at Sasha.

"Oh I hope so."

"There won't be any cars around this area at this time of night."

"I've noticed," said Sasha.

"Okay, here's your drop off spot. Go have fun."

Sasha snorted. "Fun! I hope so."

She quietly got out of the car and closed the door without a sound. She pulled her hoodie up and walked quickly to the building. She couldn't believe her luck when the streetlight at the corner was out. Stealthily she moved with purpose until she was pressed up against the building. She slowly peeked around the corner and could see

Noelle at the other end of the building looking away from her.

As Sasha got closer her heart began to beat out of her chest. She was beginning to doubt that this was a good idea when Noelle slowly turned and saw her coming.

“What are you doing?” she whispered. “I thought you were coming from the other...” She never finished her sentence as realization set in.

Sasha could see the surprise on her face. “Let me explain,” she said softly.

“Sasha, what are you doing here?”

Before she could answer, a car's lights shone directly on them. It pulled up to the curb and the driver rolled down his window.

“Hey, what are you doing over there?” a voice called.

Sasha could see the fear on Noelle’s face. She had to do something fast. “It’s okay,” she whispered.

Then she turned toward the car and said, “Shhh, we’re trying to catch the tree decorator.”

She took a few steps toward the car when the man said, “Oh shit. Is that you, Ms. Solomon? Sorry.”

“It’s okay. I would have probably stopped too. Do you mind going on? We heard they might be here and we’re trying to surprise them,” she said with authority.

“No problem. Hi Noelle,” the man said. “Good luck!”

“Hey Curtis,” Noelle squeaked.

He rolled his window up and drove away.

They both let out a relieved breath and Sasha turned to Noelle. “We’d better get with it before someone else shows up.”

“Hold on!”

“Later, Noelle. I’m taking Belle’s place. I’ve come to help you decorate. We need to hurry, don’t you think?”

Noelle stood there with her mouth open, clearly still in shock.

Sasha gave her a sweet smile and grabbed her hand, leading them towards the bag Noelle had dropped on the ground. "Show me what to do."

"Uh," stammered Noelle, then her brain seemed to clear. "I'll do the lights while you start on the ornaments."

"Okay," whispered Sasha.

They quickly went to work. Sasha hung several ornaments and would back away so Noelle could come around with the lights. When she realized a smile was on her face she turned to look at Noelle and she was smiling too.

"It's Belle's turn to put the star on," Noelle said softly.

Sasha turned to her and Noelle handed her the star. "Can you reach?"

"I think so," said Sasha. She stretched toward the top of the tree and pushed the star on the top.

They stepped back and Noelle whispered, "That's perfect."

Sasha was making sure nothing was left on the ground when she felt Noelle's hand on her shoulder. She stood up and Noelle was smiling at her.

"You should put this one on." She handed her the rainbow ornament that had been on every tree so far. "Right in front, babe. Put it right in front."

Sasha's smile could have lit the night. She took the ornament and hung it just like Noelle instructed. Then Noelle turned on the lights.

"Okay, we've got to get out of here," said Noelle. "Come with me." She grabbed Sasha's hand and pulled her towards the street. When they were hidden by the trees on the other side they turned to look at the tree.

"This is the best one yet," said Noelle.

Sasha was reminded of the ornament she'd bought their first night together of the two women looking at the Christmas tree in the woods. She could see the twinkling lights of the tree reflected in Noelle's eyes. Her heart overflowed with love for this woman.

Noelle turned towards her and seemed unable to take her eyes off Sasha.

Sasha reached up and took Noelle's chin in her hand. She smiled and said, "I love you, Noelle Winters."

Noelle's head tilted and she said softly, "I love you, Sash."

Sasha didn't think she'd ever heard anything sweeter. She leaned in and kissed Noelle tenderly with all the love that had been growing in her heart since the first moment she met her.

They reluctantly pulled away and Noelle gave her a penetrating look. "Let's go home, honey. So you can explain to me what is going on."

Sasha chuckled low in her throat and put her arm around Noelle's shoulders. They hurried to Noelle's car and got in.

"Where's your car?" asked Noelle.

"At my house. We can go there," answered Sasha.

Noelle cut her eyes toward Sasha. "You could've told Curtis about me and solved the Great Christmas Tree Mystery."

"But I didn't."

"Why?"

"Because I want to be your elf."

Noelle smiled and kept her eyes on the road.

Sasha wondered what she was thinking, but the smile told her at least she wasn't angry.

19

They walked into Sasha's house and she said, "I'll be right back."

Noelle watched her walk into the kitchen and she plopped down on the couch. So many things were flying through her head. She smiled as she recalled her shock to see Sasha under that hoodie instead of Belle. Then when Curtis drove up the look in Sasha's eyes made Noelle feel protected. They were in perfect sync as they decorated the tree unlike she and Belle had been in the beginning. She looked up as Sasha walked back into the room with two glasses of water.

She handed one to Noelle and sat down beside her. They both took a long drink and Sasha looked at Noelle expectantly, but didn't say anything.

Noelle smiled, knowing that Sasha would wait for her to speak when she was ready.

"I have so much I want to tell you, but first," said Noelle, setting her glass on the table. She turned to Sasha and smiled. "You love me," she said with wonder in her voice.

Sasha set her glass next to Noelle's and took her hands. "I do," she said. "And you love me too."

Noelle nodded. "Do you have any idea how good that makes me feel?"

"I know how good it made me feel to say it and then when you said it back," Sasha said, her voice full of love.

"I want to take you to that exquisite bed of yours and show you the love I have for you, but I need to tell you about my mom first." Noelle could see what looked like relief on Sasha's face.

"I want to hear everything, my love."

"But after," said Noelle. "I want you to tell me all about what just happened and how you figured it out."

Sasha smiled. "I will. Tell me about your mom," she said, squeezing her hand.

Noelle took a deep breath and exhaled. "I've told you that my mom always helped a family at Christmas." Sasha nodded and Noelle continued. "We kind of fell into a routine over the years. I usually had time between relief assignments to come home for a visit. Sometimes I'd be gone a few weeks and then other times it might stretch into months. I would come home and tell my mom about the people and the hardships, but also about their resilience and love for one another and us. She would tell me about the families she helped."

"So you would kind of unload with her," commented Sasha. By this time they had sat back on the couch and Sasha had her arm around Noelle, gently rubbing her shoulder.

"Yes. I could get out all the sadness, but also share the happy moments too. She would tell me about all the members of the families and explain what she did. We swapped stories. You know, people don't realize what a little help can do. Just a hand here or there can make such a difference."

Sasha nodded and waited for her to continue.

"When Mom died I stopped talking about my trips. All this sadness has built up inside me and I don't know what to do with it," she admitted with tears in her eyes.

Sasha turned to face her. "I'll swap stories with you. If anyone can understand those places it's me."

"What do you mean? We'll take an evening and swap a few stories and then what?"

"We won't do it all at once. That would be too much," said Sasha. "We'll do a little at a time, just like you did with your mom."

"You'll be my outlet?"

"I'll soothe your soul, like your mom did. If you'll let me."

"What happens after the stories?" asked Noelle.

Sasha shrugged. "Whatever you want."

Noelle leaned in and kissed Sasha softly. "I think you know."

Sasha brought their lips together again then deepened the kiss. Their tongues tangled, giving and receiving the love their hearts had been feeling all along.

"Mmm," moaned Noelle. "I could kiss you all night," she said, nuzzling Sasha's neck.

"Tell me more about your mom," whispered Sasha.

Noelle looked into her eyes and then sat back. "It surprises me how much I miss her. I thought it would get easier, especially with all the death I've seen through the years. I thought I would handle it better," she said, choking back a sob.

Sasha put her arms around Noelle and held her close. "It's okay," she cooed softly.

"I've seen so many strong people have to overcome such tragedy. That's what I did! I tried to make it easier for them. But when it came to my own loss I couldn't bear it. There are so many things I want to ask her and I want to tell her I love her."

"Oh baby, she knows you love her," soothed Sasha.

"I realized that I couldn't face this town without her in it. So I would flit in for a quick visit and then run away. After this visit I planned on not coming back, but then something happened." Noelle gently stroked the side of Sasha's face.

Sasha didn't say anything, just raised her eyebrows in question.

"The evening we walked the square and stopped in the shops, I felt like I could take a deep breath again. I remembered buying ornaments with my mom and instead of bringing tears, it made me smile. The more time I spent with you the more memories I began to see differently. They were happy, no longer sad."

"Oh baby," murmured Sasha.

"It's a good thing." Noelle smiled then narrowed her eyes. "But I want to know how you figured out it was me."

Sasha sighed. "Okay. But first I have something for you." She got up and went to where her purse sat on a chair. She got something out of it and came back to sit next to Noelle. She handed her the glove she'd found under the decorated Christmas tree in the park.

Noelle grinned. "Where'd you find this?"

"I found it under the tree in the park the day I went to get you mistletoe. The mysterious tree decorator left it under the tree," she said with a pleased look on her face.

Noelle gasped. "No way! We never leave anything behind!"

"You did that night, darling."

"You didn't know it was mine."

"Don't you remember when I came to your house and found your glove on the floor? I also noticed you had several unopened Christmas decorations stashed in a sack in that little storage cabinet."

Noelle nodded. "I remember. So why didn't you say anything?"

Sasha laughed. "I was too distracted by someone to put it together then."

"What?"

"If you couldn't tell, I was kind of into kissing you at that point."

Noelle grinned. "Oh I noticed!" She leaned in and kissed Sasha with a loud smack. "Go on," Noelle urged her.

"I kept thinking about what you said about the person wanting to stay anonymous, so solving the mystery wasn't a top priority. Especially when all I could think about was you," Sasha said as her eyebrows crept up her forehead.

"You're all I could think about, too," said Noelle.

"When I watched the video from the night of the School Board meeting I immediately knew," she said.

"You did?"

"Yes! I know you and all the ways your body moves! Then there were things you said, like your mom would have loved that tree. There were the rainbow ornaments that you put on our trees. You had a guilty look on your face a couple of times when Christmas trees were brought up, too."

"My gorgeous love, the question becomes what are you going to do with this information?" Noelle asked, staring into Sasha's beautiful brown eyes. She couldn't believe this woman loved her.

"I've already told you, *my* gorgeous love. I want to be your elf. I want to decorate the trees with you."

Noelle considered the meaning behind Sasha's words but before she could say anything Sasha asked, "How did you come up with this idea?"

"One night I was working at the Christmas tree lot when a delivery came in right before closing. I was the only one there and the store was already locked. I didn't want to unlock the store and have to disarm the alarm so I loaded the boxes in my SUV. They were full of ornaments and lights. I was on my way home and driving through the square when I saw a sad little tree. It reminded me of how I felt. I remembered the decorations in the back and decided I could at least cheer up this little tree. So I got out and decorated it with a few ornaments and a string of lights. Before I got back in the car I stopped and looked at it. I was surprised at how it lifted my spirits, but it also reminded me of decorating our family tree with my mom. The next day all the town could talk about was the little tree on the square that someone mysteriously decorated and it showed how special Santa Junction was. A few days later I did another one and I could feel my mom nearby. It was then that I felt like I was carrying on her work in a way. Decorating a random tree had somehow brought holiday cheer to the town."

"Noelle! That's beautiful! No wonder you want to stay anonymous. It's like you're sharing a special moment with your mom that the whole town benefits from."

"That's a perfect way to describe it," said Noelle.

"You know, I understand more of this than you think. You talked about being surprised at how hard losing your mom is on you. In the same way, it surprises me how much being part of a town like this means to me. My brother and sister seem to be fine with their lives and our nomadic childhood didn't affect them the way it did me. I can't shake the idea that I'll never belong anywhere."

"You belong here, Sash, with me," Noelle said earnestly.

"What? I thought you wanted to leave."

"That was before Santa Junction worked its magic on me. Or was it you?"

"As much as I want to belong here, Noelle, I'd go anywhere with you. If you don't want to stay here, I'm okay with that. Because where I belong is with you." Sasha ended this conversation with a scorching kiss.

When they finally pulled apart, Noelle said breathlessly, "That's quite a statement."

Sasha got up, pulling Noelle with her. "We can talk about it tomorrow. Right now, I've got love I need to give you."

They left a trail of clothes down the hallway as they ended up in Sasha's big bed. Noelle's heart was full of love and Santa Junction felt like home again.

20

The next morning Sasha slowly began to wake. She felt Noelle's arm wrapped around her middle and scooted back. Sometimes she couldn't get close enough to this woman that not only made her cry out in ecstasy, but also made her want to share every part of being. She had always held back a piece of herself in relationships because she was unsure of where she belonged. It wasn't lost on her that it could be a who not a where, but she still held back. Now she knew why.

This was where she belonged; she felt it in her soul. The longing was gone. She wasn't afraid to tell Noelle, either. Her final statement last night had made that clear. What surprised her was how this felt. It was like a calm came over her, but also her heart beat with such joyful anticipation.

Everything was so clear now. Worries of this being too fast were gone. Of course it was fast, their hearts had been waiting for this and when they finally met they were one. They didn't have to get to know one another, they already did. Sure, there are day to day things they would discover about one another, but they *knew* each other in their hearts and in their souls.

"Mmm," murmured Noelle as she kissed Sasha's naked shoulder. "I love you," she whispered. "Did you know that?"

Sasha chuckled. "I do know that." She rolled over to a sleepy-faced Noelle. "And I love how you show me."

Their lips met in a sweet, soft kiss as they pulled each other closer. The kiss deepened when their tongues touched and Sasha felt the familiar warmth spread through her that always seemed to follow a thought or a touch from Noelle.

When they pulled away Sasha looked into Noelle's eyes and said, "Thanks for sharing about your mom last night."

"I felt such relief saying it out loud. I feel safe with you."

"You are."

Noelle smiled. "Let's talk about the bold statement you made last night and then kissed me silent."

"I couldn't wait any longer to touch you." She sighed. "The last few days I've realized some things and I'm not afraid to be honest with you."

"Care to share what things?"

Sasha smiled. "All this time I thought I wanted to belong somewhere. When I came to Santa Junction I immediately felt welcomed and thought this might be the place. And as you said last night, then something happened."

Noelle raised her eyebrows and waited. Sasha could see the love in those green eyes. Love that was for her.

"It wasn't Santa Junction where I belonged; *you* are where I belong."

"But I thought you liked it here."

"I do, but I like you more," she said earnestly. "I knew all along that you wanted to leave. When Rita said I could give you a reason to stay I thought that was romantic and all, but the magic, our magic, isn't Santa Junction. It's us."

"You don't think it's magical here? Are you sure my mom didn't send you to me somehow?"

"I'll admit at first I thought this was going way too fast and then I stopped and looked at how many things had to align for us both to end up here at the same time. Maybe it's your mom or maybe it's Santa Junction. It doesn't matter. You and me together, that's what matters."

"What if I wanted to stay in Santa Junction?"

"What do you mean? Quit your job?"

Noelle looked into Sasha's eyes. "Before I came home this time, I told them I was done."

Sasha sat up in bed. "But you said you were leaving."

"I know," Noelle said, pulling Sasha down on top of her. "But things have changed."

"What were you going to do if you hadn't met me?"

"I wasn't sure. I could stay with my company in an administrative role, but I wasn't going to."

"I meant what I said last night, Noelle. I'll go wherever you want. There is no reason we have to stay here if it makes you sad."

"That's the thing, babe," said Noelle. "When I'm with you, the memories I see of my mom are happy again. I want to show you places and things that remind me of happy memories. I didn't even realize I was already doing it."

"What?" asked Sasha, confused. She propped her head on her hand and stared down at Noelle.

"Having hot chocolate on the square is something my mom would take Nick and me to do after our dad died. That's the first thing I took you to do. Then we went to the park that night to catch the tree decorator."

"You must have gotten a laugh out of that," said Sasha.

"Not at all. Belle and I planned to do that tree that night

and I couldn't figure out how someone knew. Did they really leave a tip on your website?"

"Yes! The next day I had our IT people try to see where it came from, but they couldn't tell."

Noelle furrowed her brow. "Hmm, it sounds like magic." She paused then continued. "One evening after we had swapped a couple of particularly tragic stories, my mom wanted to take a walk in the park. I remember her saying to me that it would be something romantic to do with my girlfriend one day. I hadn't thought about that until a few days after our walk."

"Maybe your mom does have something to do with this." Sasha's eyes sparkled with delight. "What else?"

"I have all kinds of happy memories of the Christmas tree lot. But the best one is when you bought your little imperfect tree and together we made it perfect."

"We did," said Sasha.

Noelle pulled Sasha down for a kiss that was full of love.

"What now?" Sasha asked.

"There is one more tree left to decorate this year," Noelle said with a twinkle in her eye. "Would you help me?"

Sasha grinned. "Are you going to let me be your elf?"

Noelle laughed. "Among other things."

"Mmm," Sasha moaned, kissing Noelle. "I think I like those other things."

"There's something I have to do first," said Noelle.

"What's that?" asked Sasha cheerily.

"I'm going to go get the high school counselor's job that happens to be open for next semester."

A smile grew on Sasha's face. "You want to stay!"

"I wouldn't want to live anywhere else. I love Santa Junction. You've given me my life back, Sasha! Besides, I can't take you away from here. Rita will never let us leave."

They both laughed and then Sasha kissed Noelle with such love.

“I finally belong!” Sasha exclaimed.

ONE YEAR LATER

Sasha walked up next to Noelle and slipped her hand in hers. "Are you thinking about your mom?"

"Yeah," said Noelle, squeezing her hand. "But they're happy thoughts. I was thinking about the day she told me this would be a romantic place to bring my girl. It's like she chose the venue for us."

"I want all your thoughts to be happy today."

"How can they not be! Have you heard that *the* Sasha Solomon is marrying a small town high school counselor?" she said in a faux gossipy voice.

Sasha chuckled. "I heard that the counselor has a heart bigger than the state and she's also very beautiful." Sasha's face softened and she leaned in and kissed Noelle softly.

"Your mom and dad told me this morning that I gave you something they never could," Noelle said with her hands on Sasha's hips.

Sasha furrowed her brow in question. "I know things you give me pretty often, but they can't be talking about that," she teased.

"I gave you a place to belong, something you'd always wanted, and they said they'd always be grateful for that."

"I will always belong right here," Sasha said, patting Noelle's heart.

"Always," said Noelle.

"Hey brides," Belle said as she walked up. "I think the whole town is here."

"We're a pretty big deal," teased Noelle.

Belle laughed. "You have no idea, but before I forget—where are you going on your honeymoon? You never told me."

"That's a funny story," said Sasha.

"You two always have funny stories. Let's hear it."

"We were both in Haiti after the earthquake. I was only there two days, but I met the nicest people from the Virgin Islands," began Sasha.

"The day Sasha left was the day I arrived. We were probably in the lobby at the same time because I also met the same nice people from the Virgin Islands."

"They invited us to come visit St. John so we called them," said Sasha.

"They were so excited that we were getting married and told us to expect the VIP treatment," continued Noelle.

"I can't wait to see Liz again. She owns a bar named Peaches. Isn't that the perfect name for a bar in paradise?"

"I'm excited to see Riley again and meet her wife, Alex. It felt like we were family when we met them," added Noelle.

"So you're going somewhere warm," said Belle.

"Heck yeah. Winter hasn't even started here yet and it's freezing. We're ready for warm breezes and a tropical beach," said Noelle.

"And bikinis with fruity drinks," Sasha said, wiggling her eyebrows.

Nick walked up and smiled at both of them. "You both look so beautiful. Noelle, mom and dad would be so proud," he said, giving her a hug.

"You've been part of the family since the moment we met you," he continued, turning to Sasha. "But let me officially welcome you." He hugged Sasha and stepped back, smiling at them both again. "Everything's ready when you are."

Belle gave them both a hug and walked away with her dad.

"Well, my love," said Sasha. "Let's get married."

Noelle pressed their lips together for a quick sweet kiss. "I love you, baby."

"I love you," whispered Sasha.

They walked across the clearing hand in hand toward the tree that Noelle and Belle had decorated the year before. This time it was decorated with all the rainbow ornaments from last year's trees along with their own. The lights were twinkling as Rita waited to perform the ceremony.

They looked out over the crowd and saw their families, friends, co-workers, and even a few of Noelle's students. When they returned from their honeymoon they planned to spend Christmas with Sasha's family at her brother's house in Colorado and then get home on Christmas Eve just in time to spend it with Noelle's family. Next year they planned to host everyone at what was once Sasha's house and now theirs. Noelle had never left after Sasha surprised her that night and helped decorate the tree at the clinic.

Sasha had begun to work on her book with Noelle's help and together they had chosen a family to help this Christmas just as Noelle's mom had. They had decorated all but one tree and Belle had promised to do the last one while they were on their honeymoon because people came to

Santa Junction to experience the magic and see The Great Christmas Tree Mystery for themselves.

Rita smiled at them both and welcomed everyone. She guided them through the ritual as they both said "I do" and exchanged rings.

When it came time for their vows Noelle simply said, "While I was in Africa a priest once told me to take hold of that which is truly life."

"I'm holding on to you," Sasha said with all the love in her heart.

Their lips met in a magical kiss and the Great Christmas Tree Mystery lived on.

ABOUT THE AUTHOR

Small town Texas girl that grew up believing she could do anything. Her mother loved to read and romance novels were a favorite that she passed on to her daughter. When she found lesfic novels her world changed. She not only fell in love with the genre, but wanted to write her own stories. You can find her books on Amazon and her website at jameymoodyauthor.com.

As an independent publisher a review is greatly appreciated and I would be grateful if you could take the time to write just a few words.

On the next page is a list of my books with links that will take you to their page.

After that I've included the Prologue and first two Chapters of my other Christmas novella, *It Takes A Miracle*

I hope you enjoy it!

ALSO BY JAMEY MOODY

Live This Love

The Your Way Series:

Finding Home

Finding Family

Finding Forever

It Takes A Miracle

One Little Yes

The Lovers Landing Series

Where Secrets Are Safe

No More Secrets

And The Truth Is...

The Great Christmas Tree Mystery

IT TAKES A MIRACLE

"Is anything better than walking hand in hand with your girl admiring all the twinkling lights and Christmas decorations," Vanessa mused while bumping her shoulder against Makenna's. She would remember this night for the rest of her life. The smell of wassle drifting out of the storefront doors along with Christmas carols piped through speakers around the town square made the atmosphere festive.

Makenna squeezed her hand. "Your girl? I like the sound of that."

Vanessa pulled her behind a tree on the square and wrapped her arms around a gasping Makenna. She looked into those dark mahogany eyes and lost her breath. Their lips came together as they had so many times before. Soft full lips that she could kiss forever. When their tongues met a spark shot through her and a moan hummed deep in her throat.

"You'll always be my girl," Vanessa said breathlessly, pressing her forehead to Makenna's.

"As much as I'm enjoying this Christmas stroll, are you

ready to go? Because these kisses are like Christmas gifts and I want to open every one."

They walked hand in hand to Makenna's car and quickly got in.

"I'm so happy your grandparents are letting you spend the night with me," she said starting the engine.

"I know. Sorry I'm so paranoid about my parents finding out about us that I made you drive to another town. There's no way anyone we know would be here and I loved walking hand in hand with you tonight."

"I loved it too but your parents aren't supposed to be back until the day after tomorrow. We still have two days and lots of time to hold hands," she said grabbing Vanessa's hand.

"I'm going to be holding more than your hand later tonight," Vanessa leaned over and kissed Makenna on the cheek. "If my parents knew we were together they'd lock me up so fast it wouldn't be funny."

"I think my parents might actually be okay with it."

"Really? What makes you say that?"

"My brother likes to tease me about being gay and he told me that he thinks Mom and

Dad would understand."

"Do you think they're wondering why you haven't dated anyone since summer?"

"I told them that I fell in love with the Petty's granddaughter and only had eyes for her."

Vanessa swatted Makenna's arm, "Very funny." She caressed Makenna's hand and pressed her lips to the back of it. "Kenna, everyone may call us kids and in some ways we still are but, I know in my heart that I'll always love you. Always."

"Nessa, I'll always love you too and I intend to show you how much tonight."

Vanessa looked at Makenna's profile as she kept her eyes on the road. She imagined them both at college, no parents to worry about, just them. Happily ever after, that's what she saw.

Makenna glanced over and saw the look on her face. "What are you thinking about?"

"The future and how good ours is going to be. Don't forget we have to run by my grandparents' and get my bag. I was so excited to get away from prying eyes that I forgot it."

"It's okay. No prying eyes at my house."

"Good because I'm going to love on you all night long."

Makenna steered the car into Vanessa's grandparents driveway and her lights revealed another car.

"Oh no! That's my mom's car. What is she doing here?" Vanessa said warily. "I'll run in and get my bag. Be right back," she said kissing the back of Makenna's hand and dropping it.

Makenna had a bad feeling in her stomach. They had planned this night since Vanessa came to see her grandparents for Christmas. She thought back to this whirlwind that was Vanessa Perry and how she had blown in like a summer storm and changed Makenna's life forever. It was love at first sight, even though neither had kissed a girl. That didn't seem to matter once their eyes met and a knowing smile formed on each one's face. They had been together everyday right up until she had to leave to go home and pack for college.

She peered out the windshield and could see shadows behind the drapes she knew were in the living room. When Vanessa left for college Makenna thought she might hear from her occasionally, but she was true to her word. She called when she could and wrote her the most beautiful love letters. They emailed nearly everyday and counted down the days until Vanessa could come visit her grandparents again for Christmas.

Her anxiety grew until she saw Vanessa running toward the car. She let out a breath she didn't realize she'd been holding. Vanessa ran to her window and Makenna quickly rolled it down.

"Something weird is going on. My parents told me to pack my stuff that we were leaving in the morning." Vanessa's eyes were wide and she was breathing hard.

"What's wrong?"

"I don't know. It feels like I'm in trouble, but they haven't said anything yet. I told them I was spending the night with you, but they said I couldn't." Vanessa looked at the house and back down at Makenna, disappointment shining in her eyes.

Makenna put her hand over Vanessa's on the door frame and looked up into her troubled face.

"I'm sorry, Ken. I told them you were waiting so I ran out the door. My grandmother keeps looking at me with these sad eyes."

"I don't want to leave you. Nessa--."

"It'll be okay. I'll call you later when they explain what's going on. I'm really sorry about tonight." Vanessa pulled Makenna's hand between both of hers and looked back at the house again. She leaned down squeezing Makenna's hand, "I love you, baby. Don't ever forget that." She quickly kissed Makenna's lips then walked back to the house.

Makenna yelled, "Wait!" Vanessa turned around. "I love you too," she said just loud enough for Vanessa to hear.

Vanessa smiled and waved. Then she turned and was gone.

Waterfalls by TLC was playing on the radio when she realized tears were falling down her cheeks. And just like that the whirlwind that was Vanessa Perry stormed out of Makenna's life, taking her heart with her.

Later that night Makenna's cheery ringtone exploded into the silence of her room.

"Hello," she said hurriedly. "Vanessa?"

Vanessa whispered into the phone, "Makenna, they know. I have to make this quick."

"How do they know?"

"They snooped in my room and found the sweet card you gave me when I got here. They're taking me home tomorrow and threatened to make me live at home and go to school there. I had to promise not to see you or talk to you anymore."

"Vanessa!"

"I'm so sorry. Kenna, I convinced them that I'm not gay that it's just you so they're giving me a chance."

"A chance? What do you mean?"

"They said if I don't talk to you or see you that they'll let me go back to the university."

"What do we do now?

"I'm really scared, Makenna. I'll write to you when I get back to school. Please don't try to call me or write me at home."

"But--,"

"They're coming," she whispered. "Remember, I'll always love you, Kenna. Always." The call ended.

Makenna received one letter after Christmas. Vanessa begged her not to write or call because her parents were watching her even while she was away at college.

CHAPTER 1

Makenna could see her reflection on the computer screen. Her scowl was visible even though the monitor was darkened. She took a deep breath and willed the Christmas spirit to enter her body. When she let it out she tried to smile. What a miserable attempt.

Christmas was not her favorite time of year, and she was tired of being called Scrooge. She didn't want to be like this. It had been twenty five years since her heart was broken during the Christmas holiday and she was over it. She'd been over it for a long time or that's what she kept telling herself.

A knock on the door brought her back to her purpose. That would be Declan Sommerfield, here for his weekly check-in. She had been his counselor since he walked on campus back in August for his first semester as a student athlete at Denison University. She immediately liked the young man and couldn't put her finger on it, but there was something familiar about him. He had taken her suggestions and had excelled academically this first semester which can sometimes be difficult for incoming freshmen.

"Come in."

A tall, lanky, sandy haired young man came through the door. "Hi Coach Markus."

Makenna shook her head at the greeting. "Declan, how many times do I have to tell you I'm not a coach."

"You are to me," he said, sitting down on the couch in her office.

Makenna got up from her desk and came around to the chair opposite the couch.

"How's your week been? Are you ready for the Christmas break?"

"I'm ready for classes to be over, but you know I'll have practice during the entire break."

"You'll get some time off. I thought you were going home for Christmas," she said, a bit concerned.

"I was, but my mom has decided to come here for the holidays," he said, seeming unaffected.

"Are you disappointed you're not going home?"

"Not at all. Christmas has never been a very cheery time around my family."

"Really? I can relate. It's not my favorite."

"I got my grades in all but one class. I'll take that final tomorrow and then I'll be finished," he said happily.

"How did you do?"

"Don't you know?"

Makenna chuckled, "I could check, but I know you'll tell me. So, how did you do?"

"I have a B in Calculus and A's in everything else."

"That's awesome, Declan!" She got up and high-fived him.

"I should get an A in Creative Writing tomorrow unless I blow the final and I don't see that happening."

"I'm really proud of you."

Declan's smile beamed on his face. He didn't know why her opinion meant so much to him, but it did. "I couldn't have done it without you. Seriously *Ms.* Markus," he said emphasizing the Ms.

Makenna laughed and shook her head. "You know you can call me Makenna."

"I know. It's too much fun keeping you guessing."

This kid Makenna thought.

"I'll be here over the holiday if you need me."

"I'm sure I will. Do you do family counseling too? My family could probably use it."

Makenna furrowed her brow. He'd never mentioned problems with his family although he did tell her his parents were divorced and had been since he was four.

Declan noticed her concern. "It's okay. Hopefully it'll be me and my mom for the holidays. I'm sure my dad will spend the entire time with my other family. And Mom won't invite my grandparents, which I consider a gift."

"You don't get along with your grandparents?"

"Not really. It's more that my mom doesn't get along with them. They can be demanding and if you don't do things their way then it's not pretty. She wised up and the two of us do our own thing now."

"You're not staying in the dorm are you?"

"No. My mom was rather vague, which isn't unusual when talking about our family. But, we're staying in a house that belongs to her somehow or another," he said murmuring at the end.

"Okay," Makenna said, nodding her head trying to follow his ramblings. "At least you won't be in the dorm."

"And my mom is a great cook so she'll be making me all sorts of treats and feeding me well. She makes the best pecan pie. I'll get her to make you one."

"How nice, Declan. But you don't have to do that."

"I'm telling you Coach, it's the best pecan pie you'll ever taste," excitement covered his face and his eyes twinkled.

Those eyes and that smile touched a memory in the past that Makenna couldn't quite bring forward. It made her smile though and she could feel his happiness.

"That's certainly filled you with the Christmas spirit."

He looked around the room and then eyed her. "There's not much of it around here."

She looked around and saw how devoid her office was of Christmas decorations unlike the hall outside and the rest of the building. "What do you mean, there's a snow globe right there on the table in front of you."

Declan smirked and picked it up and shook it. "That's what I like about you. You're authentic and honest. Why decorate with a bunch of stuff if you don't feel it." He set the globe down, "Seriously Makenna, I hope you have a happy holiday."

His candor made her smile and sit back in her chair. There was that twinkle in his eyes. "Thank you Declan."

She looked down at her notes and back up at him, the moment passed. "What do you have the rest of the day?"

"I have a little studying to do for tomorrow and then I'm packing a bag. My mom will be here tonight."

"All you have tomorrow is the one final?"

"Yes, but I also have a workout right down the hall in the weight room. I'll stop in and say hi. Hey, did I see you cranking on the spin bike the other day in the all purpose room?"

"You may have," she answered evasively then chuckled.

Declan laughed. "We should go run sometime."

"Oh, I don't think so. I couldn't keep up with you."

"I'll go slow," he offered.

"Listen, even though there aren't any classes, I'll be in and out. So if you need me, call or text."

"Thanks. You're not going skiing or seeing your family?"

"My family is right here so no. I'm staying."

"Okay. I'll text you when Mom makes your pie," he said getting up.

"Good luck tomorrow," she said, walking him to the door. "Oh wait." She walked over to her desk and picked up a bowl of Christmas candy.

"Here," she said, offering him the bowl. "I have a little Christmas cheer. Take all you want."

"Candy canes are my favorite," he said, taking several from the bowl.

"Bye Declan."

He smiled and took off down the hall.

Makenna closed her door and shook her head. If she ever had a son she'd want him to be like Declan Sommerfield.

CHAPTER 2

Vanessa walked around the house as memories wrapped around her like a warm shawl. She could smell her grandmother's famous chocolate chip cookies cooling on the kitchen counter. As she walked through the living room she could hear the news on the TV that her grandfather watched every night. She remembered it came on at five, then five-thirty and then at six and she asked him why he watched it three times. Smiling, she could hear him say, "It takes three times for it to soak in."

Then she walked down the hallway to the room she slept in when she visited. Memories of Makenna nearly knocked her down. She remembered sitting on the bed and stealing a kiss fearful her grandmother might walk in. The butterflies from all those years ago were fluttering again in her stomach because what she remembered next took her breath away.

Makenna had spent the night. When they were sure her grandparents were asleep they explored one another's bodies with tentative kisses and touches at first. But their courage grew with each quiet moan and their labored breathing. She could still feel the velvety softness of Makenna the first time she slid her finger inside. How could she still remember that? Surely it was because she was standing in the room where it happened.

She heard a car pull into the driveway. Shaking herself out of the past she walked to the living room and looked out the window. A smile grew on her face as she recognized her son's car. She opened the front door and waved.

He had a bag thrown over his shoulder as he returned her smile. "Hi Mom," he said, opening his arms for a hug.

"My boy!" she exclaimed and wrapped her arms around his waist and pulled him tight.

"Mom, really? Boy."

"Come on Declan. You'll always be my boy. And I'm happy to see you," she said, walking him into the house with her arm still around his waist.

"Wow!" he said, looking around. "Dated much."

Vanessa chuckled,"I know. I opened up a few windows earlier so it could air out some but it got chilly in here."

"So explain to me again how this is your house."

"Well, my grandparents, Gran's mom and dad, lived here. I came to visit summers and holidays when I was younger. I spent the entire summer here right before I went off to college."

"How horrible was that?" he asked, walking around the living room looking at the old pictures on the end tables.

She laughed and then quieted, "It wasn't horrible at all. It was one of the best summers ever."

Declan looked at her curiously as her voice trailed off. "Mom? What was so great?"

Vanessa brought herself back to the present. "Oh, you know how your Gran is. I was away from her, that's what made it great."

"I can definitely understand that," he laughed with her.

"So, enough about the past. Do you have to study?"

"Nope I looked over everything for tomorrow's final after my counseling appointment this afternoon. That reminds me, would you make my counselor one of your awesome pecan pies. I couldn't have made it through the semester without her."

"Is this the academic counselor your coach set you up with that you're always talking about?"

"I'm not always talking about her. She was really helpful with adjusting to college life and athletics. It was really stressful there for awhile. But with her help I should bring home all A's and one B."

"Way to go honey. I'm proud of you."

"Thanks Mom. So will you bake her a pie? I told her how good yours are."

"I'd be happy to. But tonight we're eating out because there's no food in this place. I'll go to the grocery store tomorrow."

"Works for me."

"This is your turf so you pick. What do you want to eat?"

* * *

Makenna pulled into her driveway and saw a black blur dart across the yard. She smiled knowing it was one of her two cats welcoming her home even though she was a little later than usual. A quick workout had turned into a longer one when she felt like she was 'in the zone'. She chuckled to herself recalling Declan Sommerfield's invitation to run with him.

She walked into the house as the blur scurried through the opened door. A chorus of meows greeted her as she closed the door and walked into the kitchen. "My goodness you act like I never feed you. Come here Tina, you beautiful ball of fur." The cat came over and walked between her legs as Makenna bent down and pet her. She was a black fluffy cat with orange and red highlights. Makenna had never seen another cat look like her.

She purred with every stroke until she was bumped out of the way by a bigger yellow and white cat. "Max, don't be mean to your little sister." Makenna pet them both to growls and purrs. "Okay, here's your food." She filled both their bowls and watched them for a minute. "I'm the typical lesbian with cats," she said out loud and laughed at herself.

She looked in her refrigerator and found nothing to make much of a dinner for herself. Next she opened the pantry and didn't find anything there either. She released a big breath and walked back to her room to change clothes. She threw on a sweatshirt and a pair of joggers and put her hair in a ponytail and pulled it through her favorite cap.

On the way back to the kitchen she stopped at the hall closet and pulled out a coat. "I'll be right back, kids. Momma needs some supper."

She could hear a noodle bowl with sweet and spicy cauliflower from her favorite Vietnamese restaurant calling her name. Her favorite place was in an area full of restaurants and nightlife so she called her order in on the way. All she'd have to do is hop out, run in and pick it up.

A car was backing out just as she pulled into the area of the restaurant and she felt fortunate because they were busy tonight as people meandered up and down the walkway. She jumped out, locked her car and ran into the restaurant.

The aromas that assaulted her nose made her stomach growl.

"Hi Makenna. How are you this evening?"

"Hey Jason. I'm hungry and wanted you to cook for me tonight."

"I'm happy to do it," he said laughing. "Let me get your order."

"Thanks." She looked around and saw a few students that she recognized from campus. The live music in the background almost made her want to stay for a while.

"Here you go," he said, placing a bag on the counter as he rang up her order.

"Thanks Jason," she handed him cash she pulled out of her pocket. "Keep the rest for you."

"Aw thanks Makenna. Enjoy your evening."

"I will, now," she said her eyes wide, taking the bag and walking out the door.

She walked in front of the restaurant and was about to step off the curb when she heard, "Hey, Coach Markus!"

Makenna turned and saw Declan Sommerfield walking toward her, his face bright with a smile. A woman was just behind him trying to keep up.

"Hey Declan," she said, returning his smile.

"Hi. I'm so glad we ran into you. I want you to meet my mom," he said turning to the woman that walked up beside him.

Makenna's mouth fell open. She'd know her anywhere. It may have been twenty-five years, but the woman that took her heart was standing next to Declan. She was even more beautiful than the memories burned into Makenna's brain.

"Vanessa?" she said, not trusting her eyes.

Vanessa looked up and stopped in her tracks. "Makenna, is that you? Of course it's you!" she said suddenly breathless.

"You know each other," Declan said confused but smiling.

They were both visibly surprised, but neither said anything nor looked away.

"I can't believe it," Vanessa said softly. A smile began to take over her face as her eyes sparkled.

That's when Makenna realized why Declan's eyes felt so familiar, they were Vanessa's! And she couldn't stop looking into them. How many times had she fallen into those rich amber eyes.

Vanessa found her voice, "We knew each other a long time ago."

Makenna finally looked away and smiled up at Declan. "Showing your mom your favorite hang outs?"

"Not really. There's no food in the house."

Makenna nodded and turned to Vanessa. "Are you staying at your grandparent's place?"

"Yeah," she said softly as she tried to hold Makenna's eyes. "It's actually mine now."

Hearing this, Makenna's eyes widened. "Yours?"

"Yeah, they're both gone now and they actually left it to me."

Makenna nodded remembering Vanessa's grandparents. "I'm sorry, they were really nice people."

Vanessa nodded in agreement, but could only stare at Makenna's deep brown eyes trying to read her thoughts.

"Well, it's nice to see you again, Nessa. Good luck on your final tomorrow Declan."

"Thanks, Coach. I'll drop by and see you," he said grinning.

She turned to walk away when Vanessa reached out and gently grabbed her arm. "It was great seeing you, Ken."

Makenna couldn't help but smile, "It's good to see you too, Nessa."

Vanessa dropped her hand and Makenna walked into the parking lot.

"I can't believe you know each other. That is so cool!"

"I can't believe Makenna Markus is the counselor you've been talking about all this time," she said watching her walk to her car.

"Come on. I'm hungry."

"Me too." She followed Declan into the Vietnamese restaurant.

"Find us a seat and I'll order. Okay?'

"All right," she said looking around. "I'm going to the back."

Vanessa found them a booth and couldn't believe they'd run into Makenna Markus. For so many years, she dreamed of finding Makenna. All she needed was a chance. A chance to apologize for her cowardice, for not coming to find her when she finally got out of her marriage. But then she had Declan. This wasn't exactly how she may have dreamed it, but she was here and she could see with one look that Makenna Markus still loved her. All she needed was a chance.

Get It Takes A Miracle

Printed in Great Britain
by Amazon

71784698R00104